# KADEN

Boyfriend For Hire, Book 2

_____

## RJ SCOTT
## MEREDITH RUSSELL

Love Lane Books

Kaden, Boyfriend for Hire, Book 2.

Copyright 2019 by RJ Scott

Copyright 2019 by Meredith Russell

Cover design by Meredith Russell

Edited by Sue Laybourn

ISBN: 9781785645402

*RJ ~ Always for my family.*

*Meredith ~ For my family and friends for their continued love and support. And thank you to RJ for allowing me to create another beautiful story with her.*

# Boyfriend for Hire
# KADEN

## RJ SCOTT & MEREDITH RUSSELL

Love Lane Books

## Chapter One

The rich scent of coffee hung in the air, mixed with the familiar new leather scent of his cousin Gideon's office. Kaden Moore closed his eyes and relaxed into his seat beside the window. With a contented sigh, he angled his face toward the warming rays of the afternoon sun and tapped the arm of the chair in time with the ever-present ticking of the clock hanging on the wall behind him.

"You're like my cat." Gideon interrupted the rhythm Kaden had been strumming along to. "Even the smallest strip of sunlight and she'll be laid in it. Usually somewhere I end up tripping over her, the pest."

Kaden opened his eyes, blinking as the brightness caused his vision to blur. He turned to focus on Gideon, who was shrouded in darkness on the other side of the room.

"You have a cat?" Given Gideon appeared to be permanently glued to the office, Kaden wondered when he found the time to care for a pet.

Gideon owned and managed Bryant & Waites. The

boyfriend-for-hire company was his baby, and looking around the gorgeous office now his eyesight had adjusted, Kaden was reminded of his cousin's success. From the leather to the wood paneling and the crystal chandelier, it was tastefully done and a far cry from the house where Kaden had grown up. When Kaden was a child, his family had been just him and his mother. It wasn't until he was fourteen Kaden realized he wasn't as alone as he'd believed, and family had become something more. It was then that people like Gideon had come into his life, and for the better.

Gideon picked up his cup of coffee. "You sound shocked that I have a cat."

"I do?" He shouldn't have been. Kaden was aware of the time Gideon made for the people around him. He was one of them, after all. "Sorry, I didn't mean to." Kaden rested his hands over the closed file sitting in his lap and tried not to fidget. The thought of having another living being relying on him left Kaden with tightness in his chest.

"A three-year-old Ragdoll." Gideon blew the surface of his drink. "Kimi has the prettiest blue eyes. You'll have to visit one day. It's been a while."

Despite Gideon's presence in his life for more than a decade, Kaden was still in the habit of keeping him at a distance. There was also their age difference. Gideon was more than fifteen years his senior and had forged a direction for his life before Kaden was even born. Kaden couldn't help but continue to feel disconnected from the other man despite all the assistance Gideon had given him.

"Couldn't help but fall in love with her when I found her in my yard."

Kaden smiled. "Love, huh."

There was a brisk knock at the door, and Rowan Phillips, Gideon's hardass PA, leaned inside.

"I've just had the client's agent, Arthur Dennis, on the phone."

"And?" Gideon looked at him over the top of his coffee cup.

Rowan frowned as he stepped into the room. He hated anyone being late, which Kaden had learned to his cost when he'd listened to Rowan's speech about punctuality after he was caught on a broken-down train. Rowan had ended by explaining how Kaden could have called a cab after climbing out of the window of said train and that being the owner's cousin didn't give him a free ride. Yeah, he took punctuality very seriously.

"They *say* they hit some traffic." He rolled his eyes. "ETA is another ten minutes on top of the twenty minutes they've already missed by."

"Right." Now it was Gideon's turn to frown. "How greatly does that impact the rest of the afternoon?" Gideon was a man who liked order, which made him and Rowan such a good team.

"Not too badly." Rowan pushed the door closed, then made his way over to Gideon's desk. "Look." He opened the planner that Gideon kept there, and leaned forward slightly, running his finger over the page. "Darcy and Mrs. Peterson are at two, but that should be pretty straightforward as it's their fourth date now. He's her regular companion to those art functions she attends. So we should be able to make the time up there as it's a quick in and out. I'll contact them and advise them we may be running late."

Gideon glanced at Rowan, then nodded. "Thank you."

"Not a problem." Rowan smiled, his gaze lingering on the planner for a moment. With a small laugh, he switched his attention to Kaden, who was mid-yawn. "Excited as always, I see." He walked around to the other side of the desk. "This job is for a Hollywood star. Are you really not at all excited about *the* Ryan Levesque coming here? Or even a little bit interested?"

"In what?"

"Him? His characters? The bright lights of show business?" Rowan underlined that last part with jazz hands, and Gideon stifled a laugh behind his fist. "He's one young and sexy guy."

Kaden ran his fingers over the file. "You're a fan of this Ryan guy, then?" Until a few days ago the name Ryan Levesque had meant very little to him. He knew the man was an actor, had risen from a recurring role on a long-running soap opera to become a sought-after commodity, thanks to some teen fantasy movie, but that was the end of it.

"Maybe a little." Rowan folded his arms as he sat on the edge of the desk. "The soap opera he was in was somewhat of a guilty pleasure while I was between jobs. *Destiny Cove*, so bad it was good. Have you ever seen it?"

Kaden shook his head. "Can't say I have."

Rowan shrugged. "Mr. Levesque's character, Logan, was kind of fun, if not a little bit trashy as he got older. I mean, there was this whole storyline where we found out his dad wasn't really his dad. His real dad was, in fact, his grandfather. All very overdramatic with debatable acting, but I couldn't stop watching."

"I'm sorry I missed it." Kaden assumed his tone

expressed his disinterest, but it seemed Rowan saw it as something to be challenged.

Rowan smiled as he explained, "The grandfather had slept with his son's wife. And so the man that Logan thought was his dad was actually his half-brother, and his sister was therefore also his niece. And I guess it meant his mom was also his sister-in-law." Rowan raised a finger to his mouth, tapped his lower lip. "Huh."

Kaden cleared his throat. "And I thought my family had problems." He winced as the statement left his mouth, aware Rowan was then staring at him with interest.

"Is this a rare mention of the elusive Moore family?" Rowan grinned.

Kaden ran his hand back over his shorn hair, feeling the prickle against the palm of his hand.

"It suits you, by the way," Rowan changed the subject and tilted his head. "Your hair being short like that."

"You think?" Kaden lowered his hand and rested it over his other on the file. He wondered how uncomfortable he must have looked for Rowan to willingly give up his pursuit of information and instead steer the conversation elsewhere.

"I do. It's different. Though I confess, I was partial to your curls—"

"How are June's accounts coming along?" Gideon lowered his cup to the desk with a thud. He glared up at Rowan, and there was an undeniable message in the look that spoke volumes.

"I'm nearly done." Rowan checked over his shoulder. He raised an eyebrow as he met Gideon's gaze. "And I should probably get back to it." He stood straight, tugging his shirt to smooth the creases at his stomach. "I'll let you know when Mr. Levesque and his party arrive." Rowan backed toward the door.

"Thank you, Rowan."

"Yes, sir." He gave a casual salute, and the catch made a soft *click* as he pulled the door closed behind him.

"You'll have to excuse Rowan. It's that time of the month," Gideon said.

Kaden was surprised. Was Gideon trying to be funny? "Erm, time of the month?"

"Yes, when he's playing catch-up on the accounts and paperwork. He enjoys looking for distractions and stopping in the office to talk. Today you're his distraction." He met Kaden's eyes. "What did you think I meant?"

"That, obviously."

Gideon laughed. "He's right about the hair, though. It suits you. Any reason behind getting it all cut off?" Kaden's selling point had always been his messy curls. His innocent yet seductive charm from beneath long wavy bangs.

Kaden reached up to touch his hair. "I just figured a change might be for the best, considering the job. I know I'm not expected to give any direct on-camera interviews, but I'll be present for a lot of them, even if I'm just hanging around in the background."

The intercom sounded, and a crackle of interference momentarily distorted Rowan's voice before clearing. "Sir, I've just buzzed in Mr. Levesque and his associates. Should I bring them straight through?"

Gideon held down the speak button. "Yes, please." He rose and buttoned his jacket, straightening his spine.

Following Gideon's lead, Kaden placed the file on his seat and pulled at his shirt's cuffs.

What kind of man was Ryan Levesque?

Kaden had decided against putting too much time into researching the actor, had figured he would avoid wading through the media bullshit, be it positive or negative, and make up his own mind when he met Ryan in person. He had been made aware of why Ryan needed a fake boyfriend, and that it had something to do with a leaked video. For the time being he held no opinion one way or the other over its content, although he'd watched it a few times. Even good people were capable of ignorant acts and ill-thought words, especially when they were drunk as Ryan had been. He wasn't ready to crucify the man along with the online masses without getting a handle on the situation first. On the other hand, he wasn't going to excuse it.

There was a brief moment of anticipation, followed by a knock on the door.

"Come in."

Rowan held the door open as two men, and a woman followed him into the room. "Sir, Mr. Dennis, and Mr. Levesque."

"Thank you, Rowan."

The older of the two men approached Gideon's desk with his hand outstretched. "I apologize for our tardiness." He patted the breast pocket of his navy suit jacket. "Arthur Dennis." Then indicated in the direction of his male companion. "Ryan Levesque I assume you know, and this is his sister Carmen. Thank you for seeing us today." He gripped Gideon's hand and gave it a firm shake.

"Gideon, and not a problem. Please have a seat." Gideon sat.

Arthur settled into one of the chairs in front of Gideon's desk. "Ryan?" Arthur glanced over his shoulder. "Can you join us, please?"

Ryan hesitated, having chosen to hang back with the woman called Carmen. Probably in an attempt to maintain his anonymity, Ryan was wearing dark glasses, along with a hooded sweater, which cast shadows over his features.

*The woes of being a celebrity.* Being recognized entering the premises of an agency that hired out boyfriends was not what the troubled actor needed right now.

Carmen rested her hand on Ryan's shoulder to encourage him. She leaned in close to whisper in his ear. Her long blonde hair obscured both her and Ryan, and she reached up to tug Ryan's hood back. Eventually, she pulled away and gave Ryan a firm look from over the black frames of her glasses.

"Yeah." Ryan's voice was low and held an edge of weariness. "Yeah, of course." He removed his glasses and joined Arthur, then sat forward in his seat. "So how does all this work?" His voice wavered as he folded down the arms of his glasses. He held them in his lap and cleared his throat.

Gideon glanced in Kaden's direction. "Our meeting today is about introductions and working out the small details."

Kaden caught the tightening of Ryan's jaw, the way he tensed. He wasn't happy to be there; in fact, he appeared scared. He flicked his head, his long bangs parting, and stared directly at Kaden. "Are you the fake boyfriend they partnered me with?" His sharp and confident words were at odds with his guarded expression.

"I am." Kaden didn't move from his position beside the window. He felt that approaching could cause Ryan to fortify his defenses. "Kaden Moore."

Ryan looked Kaden up and down and then settled his frosty blue gaze on Kaden's. "Have you done this before?"

"Been hired to act as someone's boyfriend?" Kaden had been with Bryant & Waites for just under three years.

"I assume it's a given you're not inexperienced, but I meant someone as high profile as me?" There was defiance in Ryan's expression and haughtiness that spoke of privilege. Kaden imagined he was used to people going out of their way to reinforce his self-assessment.

"Not a high-public profile, no," Kaden admitted.

Ryan clicked his tongue and shrugged, dismissing Kaden. "You said they had someone, Arthur. It's ridiculous to expect someone with no experience with paparazzi and the pressure to be able to pull this off." He cast a quick look at Kaden, who met his gaze. His fear was more apparent.

Gideon interjected, "The fact his previous work has been of a more discreet fashion is important here and is exactly why I selected him after receiving your brief." He leaned back. "Though not a common occurrence, there are a few of our *boyfriends* who, depending on how much interest media outlets take, could be recognized from prior engagements. So I consider Kaden to be the best fit for you and this arrangement." His smile conveyed it was he who was in charge when it came to his office.

"Maybe we need to find someone else," Ryan snapped.

"I do have companies I can refer you to." Gideon remained calm. "But of course, at this late stage, you will be lucky to find someone with Kaden's credentials."

"I'm sure we can find someone," Ryan pressed.

"You can try," Kaden murmured, just loud enough for Ryan to hear.

"Do you know anything about actors?" Ryan asked, pointedly.

"Not much, no."

"And movies?"

"I've seen one or two."

Ryan was wide-eyed now. "Arthur, what did we—?"

"We take great pride in matching our clients with the right men, and you will find none finer at this point than Kaden Moore," Gideon interrupted.

Ryan opened his mouth to comment, but Carmen laid a hand on his shoulder, and Ryan sat back, abruptly subdued.

Arthur cleared his throat. "We want to thank you for your handling of this delicate situation. Understandably, it's got us all a little tense." He glanced at Kaden. "I'm sure we'll make this work."

"Totally understandable." Gideon motioned for Kaden to join them. "So, shall we begin?"

The meeting lasted an hour, and by the time they were done, they had a series of dates scheduled over the next two weeks. All opportunities for Ryan and Kaden to spend time together before the long stretch of calendared promotional interviews, photoshoots, all leading to the red-carpet premiere of Ryan's upcoming movie release. Kaden stayed quiet, interjecting when he needed to, and Ryan grew steadily more agitated as the meeting wore on. He couldn't sit still and kept stopping the meeting to confer with Arthur in low tones about imagined scenarios where it could all go wrong that everyone in the room could hear.

He was tense, his forehead creased in a permanent frown, that only eased when it was time for the meeting to end.

"Thank you for your time." Arthur shook Gideon's hand. "We'll be in touch in a couple of days." He squeezed Kaden's hand between both of his. "I appreciate your help."

Kaden smiled, his gaze was drawn past Arthur to Ryan, who was already walking out the door. "I look forward to working with you, Ryan."

The actor didn't look back.

"What do you think?" Gideon asked as soon as they were alone.

"Ryan seems… difficult." There was no denying the two of them had a long way to go. But Kaden was sure he could make it work. He just hoped Ryan would let him.

"He probably doesn't like the pressure from the studio." Gideon shrugged. "Definitely not chilled like my Ragdoll."

"Your cat?"

"Ragdolls are known for being docile and affectionate. Despite the similarities in their striking blue gazes, Mr. Levesque is quite prickly in his temperament."

Kaden caught his lower lip between his teeth. The color of Ryan's eyes hadn't wholly gone unnoticed by him. "So it wasn't love at first sight this time, then?"

Gideon chuckled. "Not for me." He patted Kaden on the back, then returned to his desk.

Kaden considered the meeting with the unsettled, twitchy actor. Ryan was hard to figure out. Yes, he was spiky, but considering what was going on with him, those prickles were probably a way of protecting himself, above anything else. The first thing Kaden needed to do was earn Ryan's trust.

*Trust, huh? How?*

## Chapter Two

"Ry! The car's downstairs," Carmen called from outside the bathroom door and startled Ryan, who'd spent the last ten minutes staring at himself and wondering how the hell everything had become this messed up. He was used to attention from his soap opera days, but his life had grown steadily more ridiculous. He'd gone from soap star to the heights of a media darling, then falling to become the subject of memes calling him a hypocrite and liar. This morning's vitriolic post on TMZ, talking about how he was letting everyone down, had sent him into a familiar tailspin, and he'd moved into the bathroom where he'd locked the door.

"I was twenty-one," he said to his reflection. Shouldn't there have been a statute of limitations on the length of time mistakes had before they lost the power to hurt? Like, there should be an arbitrary set of years, after which all the crap magically disappeared. Maybe three? That would work, given he'd just turned twenty-four and that meant the garbage at twenty-one would have gone.

*If only the memories would go at the same time.*

"Get out of the bathroom, little brother!" Carmen shouted, and Ryan knew that if he didn't get out, Carmen would break the door.

His sister was determined, and he wouldn't put it past her to call 911 and have firefighters get him out of the bathroom. She was his touchstone, the one constant he had in his life, and it was only because of her hand on his shoulder that he'd even stayed in the meeting with that Kaden guy. That was another issue, the reaction he'd had to Kaden. He wasn't the type to lose his cool, but Kaden had stared at him, judging him and appeared to find him lacking.

"I'll be there in a minute," he called back and assumed she would wait. The doorknob rattled, and he could see the lock turning from the outside. With a huff, he unlocked it and yanked the door open, faced with his sister on her knees with a screwdriver. "I'm not even going to ask."

She shook her head in disappointment, not one ounce of regret in her for trying to break into the bathroom, then held out a hand for Ryan to help her stand. "You can't stay in there all night talking to yourself." She pressed the back of her hand to her forehead and swayed dramatically. "Woe is me, all my money, and now no one loves me."

Ryan wanted to be angry with her because she was one of a handful of people who knew the real him, but he didn't have the energy, and anyway, she was right about the fact that no one loved him.

Except for the hundreds and thousands of fans he shouldn't forget, who tweeted and Instagram'd their support with #RyanIsInnocent hashtags. He wasn't innocent, he was a fucking mess, and he *had* said what people heard on the video. He'd never denied it was him. What was the point? He'd done wrong, but it was for reasons, okay? It had been *his* words, *his* voice, and the shame he felt for what he'd said weighed him down. He was an LGBTQ advocate now—at least that is what breakfast television called him—an icon for gay youth, and he'd screwed everyone over by being weak, drinking too much, and losing control.

"I'm a shallow fucked-up failure," he blurted, and Carmen raised a single eyebrow.

"Whatever," she said tiredly.

"I've let everyone down."

"No, you haven't," she snapped, then gripped the open edges of his Fendi *Monster Eyes* jacket and yanked him closer. "You have a platform, you fucked up, but you had reasons for that, and now your platform is even bigger, and you need to make sure the messages you send from now on are good ones."

He couldn't stop panicking. "The studio is going to drop me, I know it."

"They still need you for the next film after this one. They're not going to drop you."

"I guess. But what about *Paul?* His dad is working with investors on the film. What if he has an excuse to really be back in my life because of that? I mean, he already contacted me and wants me back. He honestly thinks I would want that."

She grew serious then, compassion in her expression. "And you ignored him. That's a good thing."

"But how long can I ignore him? He said he could help, that we could get through this nightmare together. He'd support me during the fallout from the video."

Carmen shook her head. "You don't need the support he's offering."

"I know. I just can't get the idea of him being anywhere near me or the movie out of my head."

"Is that worrying you? Do we need to see someone? Maybe talk to—"

"No," he interrupted. "If I see him again, then I know what to do. I'm not the confused, desperate twenty-one-year-old who said those words anymore. It's just… what if people find out about everything that happened?"

"We've been over this, Ry," she said and pulled him into a hug. "If the worst happens, then it won't be you who people will look at. You said you were resigned to riding this out, but if you think you can't handle the possibility that your ex-boyfriend, whatever kind of asshole he is, might be part of any of this, then we can rethink."

"And what will I do if everything goes wrong and too many people hate me for what I did? What if it's all over for me?"

She huffed and shook him a little more. "Then you and me? We'll move to Canada and open up a provincial theatre and act out the plays we used to do when we were kids, and we'll be damn happy. Okay?"

Carmen was the voice of reason, saying enough for Ryan to get his thoughts in order. If he left now, if the studio fired him over a youthful indiscretion, then he'd lose his position to effect change, and everything he'd done so far would be wasted. No one had to know about Paul or what Ryan had lived through for two years and how long it had taken him to break the cycle of him and Paul. But like a bad penny, every so often Paul found a way to encroach on his world, looming over him like an oppressive shadow, dulling anything good in his life.

*And he's back again.*

No, just because Paul's father was loosely linked to the studio, it didn't mean Paul would be anywhere near any of it. Ryan needed to think positively.

If only they knew who'd sent the video to TMZ and who the hell had recorded the cell footage of him losing his head at a party? *Who had been there that night?* If only it had been an ordinary night, then it would have been Paul or maybe his best friend at the time—Luke—but neither of them would have anything to gain by releasing footage where he'd ranted about a nameless boyfriend. Paul would know it was him who Ryan had been talking about. As for Luke, he'd been as drunk as him on the night of the video and probably didn't even remember it.

Ryan had watched the footage so many times, looking for clues as to who had recorded his rant, but it could have been any one of a hundred people at his twenty-first birthday party. From the cast of *Destiny Cove* to strangers.

"Okay," he murmured, pushing back the mess in his head.

She hugged him. "Stop worrying," she added because she always wanted the last word. Then she straightened his jacket and patted his cheek. "You look very handsome."

Ryan checked out what he was wearing one last time: black slacks, a crisp white shirt, and an expensive jacket. He was every inch the reserved, young but sophisticated star that the studio needed him to be right now. Good enough to be on display again tonight at a private party in New York's exclusive Chelsea neighborhood, just another step in fixing the past mess.

"I should have stayed on *Destiny Cove*; it was easier there."

Carmen smiled, then said, "You were lucky to get out before the alien dinosaur baby storyline, which you know would have deteriorated into Dino-porn, where you'd forever be known as the T-Rex of handjobs."

Ryan blinked at her, not quite following her train of thought, even though he was used to her by now. "Dinoporn," he murmured.

"Yep, I can see it now"—she drew an arc in the air —"in lights, Ryan Levesque in *Revenge of the Dino-Porn Star*." She laughed, and it was so infectious that Ryan forgot for a moment what tonight was meant to be— step one in the rebuilding of his career.

"I love you, sis," he said and hugged her to him. She bussed his cheek, then stood back, eyeing him critically.

"Go get 'em."

All Ryan could think was that he wished she was going with him.

The car the studio had arranged was a sleek black limo with champagne on ice in the back, along with two glasses, and Ryan was tempted to open it and inhale the contents, just to take the edge off. When he was at the event, it would circle and park somewhere, ready to pick him and his date up at the end of the evening. Maybe he should save the champagne for when they were heading home.

"Good evening, Mr. Levesque," the driver said with a smile as Ryan eased himself in.

"Hi."

"Sir, could I just check the address you want me to

pick up your date from?" He gave the address.

"That's right."

Why was the driver asking? What was wrong with there? Were there gangs? Why would Bryant & Waites match him with someone in a gang, who lived in a shady part of town, with knives, and guns?

He was getting ahead of himself. "Why? What's wrong with it?" he asked on one breath.

The driver met his gaze in the mirror. "It's a mainly business area."

*Fuck, I'm losing it.*

The neighborhood they ended up in was respectable, a mix of brownstones converted into offices and a couple of glass high-rises, all jumbled together with not one gang sign in sight. Although Ryan doubted his sheltered upbringing would allow him to recognize a gang sign. It made sense that the driver would double-check because he was right. This wasn't a residential area as such, just businesses, all closed and dark, now it was eight p.m.

He pulled out his cell, checking the address, ready to call Carmen and ask if she'd written it down wrong, and then he saw Kaden, and his mouth dropped open.

The tall man was good-looking—that much Ryan had noticed in the office—but this vision striding from a side doorway of the glass office tower was way past handsome. This was sex on legs. This was confidence all wrapped up in dark pants and shirt, a jacket on his arm, and the swagger. *Oh, god, the swagger.*

"Fuck me," Ryan murmured as Kaden drew nearer. The driver got out and opened the door for him, and in a smooth move, Kaden was in the back, filling the car with his presence. This wasn't the slightly bored and judgmental man Ryan had met in the office; this was focus and sexy and *everything* incredible.

"Hey," Ryan said, then cleared his throat when the word came out as little more than a squeak. "Hey," he repeated in his normal voice.

"Hey," Kaden said back. "So, give me the lowdown on tonight."

That didn't make sense, and Ryan shook his head. "You had the briefing," he began, but Kaden held up a hand to stop him.

"I want to know your point of view. Talk me through this."

Ryan checked his watch. They were probably no more than twenty minutes out from the venue, and that didn't leave long for complicated, drawn-out feelings and thoughts.

"Okay, where to start…" He tapped his leg and considered the best angle to come at this from. "Imelda Cochrane, she plays my aunt in the movie, the one who everyone thinks is the good one but who ends up…" He waved his hand to indicate the evil side of the character. "It's her fiftieth birthday, and she's hired out the entirety of Bagatelle for a party. All the usual suspects will be there, the entire cast, half of whom aren't talking to me, and the other half who love the fact that I'm in the middle of all this shit because it means the spotlight is off the things they've done." He drew a breath when the words stopped coming. "Imelda is okay though, motherly, but she helped me out a lot, and I love her for it. Uhmmm… what else do you need to know?"

Kaden leaned over and pressed a button for the privacy screen to go up. It was dark glass, and for a moment, mesmerized by its movement, Ryan wondered if two men could get away with mutual blow jobs in complete privacy. At that thought, he grew hard in his pants, and that was not happening here and now. Thankfully Kaden's next words were enough to defeat any rising desire.

"I didn't mean the party, Ryan. Tell me about the video."

*Fuck. He went there.*

"I assume you've watched it." Suddenly, the car seemed too small a space to be locked into with someone who wanted to rake up the past, and Ryan felt hot.

"Yes, I watched it," Kaden began. "You threatened someone *because* of their sexuality, called that person a coward, and pointed out bluntly that you didn't want to be anywhere near *someone like him*. Then you threatened you'd make sure everyone knew he was gay, that you would, without reservation, *out him*, even if it meant it *destroyed him*. Tell me if any of this doesn't sound right or if I'm using the wrong words here."

Ryan wanted to sink through the seat, fall onto the road, and vanish. The way Kaden was judging him made him burn with self-pity and shame.

"Well, fuck," he said. Kaden didn't turn away, and Ryan felt like a bug on a pin, squirming and desperate. "Do we have to do this now?"

Kaden checked his watch. "We have a while, and I don't think it's right we get out at Bagatelle until you've explained what made you say all of that."

Ryan grew hotter, this time with anger. "Now, hang on a minute. I don't have to do anything. I hired *you* to do a job."

"You did, and it was to convince the world you aren't

what a lot of people are saying you are. I'm damn good at my job, Mr. Levesque, but right now, before we convince the world, I'd like you to convince me you're not the homophobic two-faced asshole the media is exposing you as."

"What? You can't talk to me like that. Who do you think you are?"

Kaden looked at him. "Quite simply, I'm the man you hired to save your career after you completely fucked up."

"Well, what happened back then is off-limits," Ryan snapped, then crossed his arms over his chest and sat back in his seat. "This conversation is over."

Kaden nodded, then lowered the privacy screen. "Driver, can you drop me here."

Ryan sat upright. "What?"

"You don't need me," Kaden said as the limo slowed.

Ryan leaned forward. "Excuse us a minute," he said to the driver and raised the divide. "I do need you. I paid for your time." *Please don't go.*

"I want to remind you that the contract states either party can cancel within twenty-four hours of the first meeting. I don't think we are a good fit."

The limo came to a full stop, and Kaden had his hand on the door handle before Ryan even had time to think.

"Wait, I'm sorry. Look, it's difficult, okay, but I don't have long to do this. Look, I'll try."

Kaden took his hand off the handle and turned in his seat. "Okay, then." He opened the screen one more time. "Driver, you can carry on. Thank you and sorry about that."

"Not a problem, sir."

Kaden secured their privacy, and then it was just the two of them alone in the back, and Ryan felt raw and exposed, but he had to try and explain without giving too much of himself away.

"I was drunk, and I know that isn't an excuse."

"You meant what you said, though."

Ryan closed his eyes. "No, I would never expose a secret like someone's sexuality. I couldn't do that to someone. Everything was wrong that night." The memory of old hurts gripped him, and his chest tightened.

"Then who shared the video?" Kaden leaned forward. "Was it you? Is this some kind of publicity stunt?"

Ryan's eyes flew open. "Christ, no."

"Okay, Ryan, none of this makes sense."

"You're telling me," Ryan muttered to himself. "What I said that night, it was like it wasn't me. Only when I'm in bed the knowledge that I said all that stuff is right there stopping me from sleeping. Maybe they were the only moments of real clarity I've had in my entire fucking life."

"Okay. Say I believe you didn't mean what you said—"

"I didn't."

"You don't deny you said the things recorded, though."

"I don't deny that at all."

"So the intention was still there. You were going to out someone against their wishes if they didn't do what? Give you money? Make your career? Was it blackmail? Why did you record it and what was the threat for?"

"My protection," Ryan blurted before he even realized what he was going to say. "And I didn't record it. I don't know who did."

"Protection from whom?"

Ryan's chest tightened. No one who'd asked that had gotten a real reply. Very few people knew the Ryan from back then. Was Kaden deserving of Ryan's honesty? Would he really walk out and leave Ryan to face the wolves alone if Ryan refused to talk?

"My boyfriend at the time," Ryan said quietly. "I'd only been with him a year, and at first it was great. I was only twenty when I met him, but I felt I was in love."

Ryan wanted Kaden to understand.

"You've only seen part of the video. You haven't seen the parts where I explain why I'm saying it all, about how weak I felt being with this man I'd fallen for."

Kaden didn't say anything, so clearly that wasn't enough of an explanation.

"His name was Paul, and I thought, for too long, I thought he was... look... he wasn't a nice guy, okay." Memories flooded Ryan, and he swallowed the grief. "It was a confusing time. I didn't get what he was doing. It took me a lot longer to understand he manipulated me. Hell, I'm not sure if I even do now. I was in a bad place, and he was so wrong. Fuck, this is hard."

"Paul. Okay, we have a name. And your intent was to what? Get a threat recorded that meant you'd be able to leave him."

"You're not listening. I never meant anyone to hear what I said. I didn't *know* it was being recorded."

"You realize nothing is safe when everyone has cell phones. You're clearly off your head drunk, at a party

with a lot of people, and you didn't think anyone would
be recording your rant?"

Ryan huffed. "Well, I get that now."

Kaden stared at him steadily. "Is this ex out of your
life now?"

"Shit, yes. I don't want anything to do with him."

"Do you think he was the one who leaked the
video?"

That was a question that Ryan had no answer to.
Who would want to rake this up after all this time?

"I don't understand why he would."

"Okay, so can you tell me more about Paul?" Kaden
encouraged, with a tiny hint of what sounded like
compassion in his voice. Maybe Kaden wasn't a hardass
who wanted to pick at Ryan's bones.

"He's openly bisexual, but his fancy-ass family would
have been mortified their only son and heir was seeing a
man. What no one sees from that single rant from me is
the stuff he did to me: threatening *me* but also
apologizing, convincing me that the pain I felt or the
anxiety that was inside me was all in my head. It was so
easy to win me back. It was part of the cycle of things.
He had girlfriends to appease his family, but he had me
warming his bed. He kept me a secret, and it was
empowering him as much as it was hurting me. Do you
know how many counseling sessions I had to attend to
know this? Too many to count."

*And I believed he loved me.* Ryan considered how he had
been at twenty-one when he'd used writing his thoughts
in a journal to make sense of his life. Thank fuck he'd
destroyed all of those a long time ago. He didn't want
anyone knowing how isolated he'd felt then. He'd still
had some confidence left, but the guilt at what he'd said

on the video and the memories of the way Paul had influenced his thoughts just left him a mess.

"Look, I don't want to do this anymore... I know I wanted to let Paul know that he was a bastard and that I could take back power. I was young. I couldn't talk to his face, okay? I'm not denying it was stupid to vocalize any of it, but at the time it was all I could do to work through what was happening to me. I think. I mean, fuck, I was drunk and off my head." He was done. He couldn't talk anymore, but it seemed that this was somehow enough for Kaden, who finally nodded as if he understood. "I don't want to talk about this anymore."

"Okay, then."

The car stopped outside the restaurant where paparazzi were standing with their cameras, and people were milling around, only a velvet rope holding them back. There were kids there who by rights should have been at home, not holding signs professing their love for Ryan or one of the other actors there tonight.

"Are you doing this with me?" Ryan asked, hating how needy he sounded.

"Yes. Are you ready?" Kaden asked.

Ryan was unsettled by how quickly Kaden switched back to his focused, all-about-business mode. "I guess I have to be."

The driver opened the door, and Kaden was out first, turning his back to the crowd and offering a hand to Ryan.

Ryan took it, and Kaden tugged him close, whispering in his ear, looking to the world as if he was kissing Ryan's cheek.

"Let's do this thing."

# Chapter Three

The party was about to enter its third hour, and Kaden was feeling the strain of making small talk in a world he knew very little about. It didn't help that Ryan was fidgety and awkward. Kaden lowered his hand, brushing the back of Ryan's in an attempt at a romantic and supportive gesture.

"I'm heading to the bathroom," Ryan said and was already mid-stride before the statement had registered with Kaden, leaving him little time to react.

He clutched Ryan's wrist, which halted him for a moment. "Don't be too long." He met Ryan's eyes, then leaned in to give him a peck on the cheek. "I'll miss you."

Ryan blinked and seemed uncomfortable, and Kaden wanted to remind him which of the two of them was meant to be the professional actor. Ryan had been on edge for most of the evening. He had his reasons to be unnerved, not knowing who had recorded the video and how much more of it was out there. Not only was it causing problems in the present, but it brought up past issues the actor had thought long buried. When the fake smiles and forced conversation faded, Ryan's expression would change. He seemed shaken, struggling to care about where he was and who he was with, and it was making Kaden's job more difficult. They were supposed to be a couple. Even if they were selling it as a new relationship, there should be some closeness there.

Ryan's body language was all wrong; affectionate interactions were far from mutual. Kaden struggled with the urge to pull Ryan close, to suggest he relax, to insist they needed to work together if they wanted to fool everybody. But it was more than that. He wanted to offer comfort, to tell him things would work out, that tonight would go as they needed it to go. However, if Ryan reacted badly, they didn't want to draw unnecessary attention to them. Kaden rubbed Ryan's shoulder, hoping to convey his concerns and boost Ryan's confidence.

It seemed to be enough as Ryan lowered his head and gave a slight nod. "I know. I know." When he lifted his head, he met Kaden's eyes with a smile that chased away the grayness of his features. "I won't be long. You'll be okay, right?" Upon entering the restaurant, they had been passed from one person to the next in a mixed string of reunions with old cast members and introductions to others from the television and movie industry. Kaden's face was aching from all the polite smiles he'd had to fabricate.

Kaden released Ryan's wrist and picked up the champagne flute from the table behind him. "I have bubbles, so I'll be fine." He took a sip, then smiled a real smile for what felt like the first time since they'd arrived. "Go on." Ryan wanted to hide for a short while. "Go do what you have to do. I'll still be here when you get back."

Ryan's features softened.

Kaden had guessed right. Ryan wanted some quiet time, and hiding in a bathroom stall was his best plan right then.

"Thanks." Ryan headed for the restrooms, glancing over his shoulder before slipping among the other partygoers.

*He'll be fine.* Kaden stared into his glass, watching the way the small pockets of air rose to break on the surface of his drink. *I'll be fine.*

When arranging meetings, this hadn't been what Kaden had had in mind. He'd imagined something more intimate in the first instance — time in Ryan's home to get to know each other better or maybe a date. Somewhere a few fans or photographers might catch them and sow the seeds of the relationship to the public. But no, here they were surrounded by people, and Kaden felt as if they were under a continual spotlight.

"Hello," someone said from beside him.

For a moment, Kaden panicked. He had let his guard down. Had his mask slipped? Had he given anything away, implied he didn't belong here or at Ryan's side?

Kaden turned his head and met the gaze of Imelda Cochrane. "Hi," he said. He kept his tone upbeat, friendly, and beamed at her in greeting. "I believe I need to wish you a happy birthday."

"Thank you." She took a drink from her large glass of red wine, her scarlet lipstick leaving a mark on the rim. "Are you okay? You were frowning."

"I was? Sorry, I'm just not used to being in the same

room as so many celebrities all at once." He glanced at the floor and blinked a few times.

"I imagine it can be overwhelming if you're not used to it. I still find myself a little star-struck at times despite having been in this industry for over thirty years." She leaned in closer. "I would say keep that last bit a secret, but I think everybody in the room knows how old I am."

"Twenty-one, right?" Kaden kept his eyes locked with hers.

"Correct answer." With a smile, she continued, "You came with Ryan, didn't you? Has he left you on your own?"

"He's just headed to the bathroom."

"I haven't had the chance to talk to him yet tonight, poor boy." She drew her gaze upward, starting from the floor. She narrowed her eyes for a moment, then met his.

Ryan had pointed Imelda out when they arrived, though, from the way the woman had been working her way around the room and how people flocked around her, Kaden would have figured it out for himself eventually.

"I'm Kaden." He held out his hand. "It's nice to meet you."

Imelda cocked her head and slid her glass onto the table. "You too, Kaden." She held his hand between both of hers. She was wearing long black gloves, silk maybe, the shiny material sweeping over his skin. "Have you and Ryan been together long?"

Kaden shook his head. He recited the details that had been agreed upon, "Not long. We met a few months back, but nothing happened until a couple of weeks ago."

Imelda shifted in her heels, and Kaden was drawn to the sway of the skirt of her black polka dot dress. "You're looking after him, right?" She squeezed his hand more tightly.

He met her gaze. The meaning of her words spanned beyond just that evening. "When he lets me."

She pouted, then released his hand. "He can be stubborn. He was always so serious on set. Of course, I appreciate the work ethic, but sometimes you have to ease off, enjoy the moment." Her features relaxed, and a hint of sadness crept into her tone. "I'm sure he must get frustrated with me sometimes. I do have a habit of mothering those I see as a little lost."

"He doesn't think that."

With a chuckle, she reclaimed her drink. "You're very sweet, but I know I can be too much for some people." She raised her glass. Before taking a drink, she said, "What can I say? I have a big heart."

Kaden tried to imagine what it must have been like for Ryan, on and off set, to have someone like Imelda take such an interest in him, want to look after him the way a mother would. That wasn't a feeling he had any experience with. Not from his mother, not from anyone else. There had been no one in his life to fill that role.

"I'm sure he appreciates you being there in his own way."

"I hope so. He's a sweet boy. I've watched him grow into a fine actor throughout these movies." Her words conveyed her fondness for Ryan. "Anyway, I should stop bothering you and get back to my other guests." She straightened the strap of her dress. "It was nice to meet you, Kaden. Make sure you look after our boy, okay?" She patted him on the chest as she moved past him.

Kaden nodded. "I will." *At least for as long as I'm hired to.*

The car was filled with a comfortable silence on the way home. Kaden rested his head against his curled fist and stared out the window. His head was woozy from too much champagne, but not so much that he didn't have his wits about him. The last thing he needed was to have fallen out of character. He watched the lights as they passed by. It wasn't just his head that felt wrong. As the streets became more familiar, the tension in his heart eased. Home wasn't far away.

"Thank you for tonight."

Kaden turned his head. Ryan sat upright, his hands clasped in his lap. The filtered glow from outside moved across his face, creating intermittent bold shadows across his features. "It's over. You can relax now." He yawned, turned back to the window, and closed his eyes.

"I mean it." Ryan breathed in loudly. "If I'd gone by myself, I don't know how I'd have gotten through the evening."

Kaden opened his eyes.

"You being there helped."

Sitting back in his seat, Kaden loosened his collar. "You'd have managed somehow. Not everyone is against you, you know?"

"Maybe." Ryan relaxed his shoulders. "But I still mean it. Thank you."

"It's what you hired me for. Though such a high-profile event straight out of the gate was quite the challenge, but I think we did okay."

Any awkwardness between them could be played off

as Kaden's shyness and unfamiliarity in a world of celebrities. Apart from a few curious stares, the night had gone smoothly.

"Do you like what you do?" Ryan asked.

Kaden shrugged. "I guess so."

"Why do you do it? Don't you find it weird pretending to be in love with someone?"

"Don't you?"

The tension in Ryan's body didn't go unnoticed by Kaden. Was it not only on-screen he'd pretended to love someone?

Kaden sighed. "You're an actor. You've played the love interest, right? It's no different, and I don't see any harm in it, not when both sides know exactly what they're getting into." He glanced at Ryan, who had turned to look out the window. "And as to why? There's no meaningful reason. I like nice things, and the job pays well." He twisted his cufflink gently.

"Nice things," Ryan repeated.

"I didn't have much growing up so…" Kaden ran his hand over his hair.

"So?" Ryan prompted.

Kaden shifted in his seat to sit higher. "So… nothing. Forget it. You wouldn't get it anyway."

"I might." Ryan had an earnest expression on his face.

Kaden scratched behind his ear. He kept his tone neutral as he asked, "Your family had money, right? A nice house and nice things, money for vacations, cars. You could ask your parents for anything and for the most part, you'd get it. Am I right?"

Ryan sucked on his teeth, probably imagining the life he'd had, his parents, his sister. "Yes."

"Then, no, you wouldn't. Not really." Kaden rested his elbow on the side of the car. He smiled. "But that's okay. You can't choose who you're born to, good or bad."

Ryan didn't say anything else, the last ten minutes of the journey returning to silence, this time a quiet that was more oppressive, stagnant.

The car pulled to a stop. "I guess this is goodnight." Kaden stared at Ryan. "Tonight went well. Rowan will be in touch with your people to make arrangements for what comes next."

"You don't want to invite me in for coffee?" Ryan suggested. He seemed serious. "It is a date, after all."

Kaden pulled his phone from his pocket and checked the time. It was already after midnight. "Sorry, but this date's over." Though he couldn't deny the request intrigued him. It had taken almost the whole night, but Ryan had eventually warmed to him, even if just a little.

The driver opened the door. "Sir."

"Goodnight, Ryan." Kaden got out of the car, then leaned down.

"Goodnight." Ryan gave him a small smile.

Kaden stood, embraced the freshness of the night air. "Night," he said to the driver and stepped back. He waited, watching until the car had pulled away and rounded the corner at the end of the street. Then the heavy weight of exhaustion and playing his part pushed his head and shoulders down. He rubbed his hand over his face and was happy to answer the lure of his bed.

Inside, he took the office block's elevator. The top two floors housed a handful of apartments, and Kaden's was situated on the highest floor.

"I'm home," he said to no one but himself as he leaned against the door to close it. He slipped off his jacket, hanging it over the back of a dining chair as he crossed the room to the large wall of glass. He rested his hands on his hips and stared beyond the buildings at the river, admiring the flicker of lights on its surface, and smiled, comforted by the vast open space in front of him. Eyes closed, he imagined himself out there, above everything, happy to be blown away on the breeze, wide and free.

It was then a memory marred the beautiful image. Harsh words, screaming, shouting, feelings of fear and guilt, followed by the sound of a slammed door and a world of darkness. Kaden opened his eyes, drank in the very real sight. He didn't need to rely on his imagination anymore. With a sigh, he kicked off his shoes. He should get some sleep. He had a debrief with Rowan in the morning, and they had to discuss the arrangements for his next date with Ryan.

*Ryan.*

Things had started on the rocky side, but they were making progress, and spending time together hadn't been the nightmare he'd feared. He could help Ryan; he was sure of that. And with that firm belief, he headed for bed.

## Chapter Four

Carmen handed Ryan a piece of paper. "This is the full list."

Ryan scanned the names, a mix of a high-end bar, a restaurant, and three clubs. He blanched at the thought of being in all those places in the space of one night. This kind of thing wasn't called a "meat run" for nothing.

Next to each place were notes.

"Restaurant, two PDA kisses, one PDA HH," he read. "What is HH?"

"Holding hands across the table, very visible, okay."

"And the PDA kisses have to be what?"

"Long and deliberate," she said and looked up from her clipboard. "At the bar, we need his arm on your shoulder and a few cheek pecks, also what will appear to others as a serious conversation. At this point, it might do well to look a little ashamed and serious."

"What will he be telling me that means I'm contrite?"

Carmen huffed. "He could be talking about the

price of sausages for all anyone knows, but the implication is that you are having a very serious chat about things." She air-quoted "very serious chat", which was awkward with the clipboard in one hand.

"Which club do I need to go to? Not all of them, right?"

"Choose one."

"And what does S-K-I-N stand for at the club?"

"It doesn't stand for anything. It's skin, show some skin, take off the jacket, expose the guns."

"What?"

She placed the clipboard deliberately onto the coffee table and cupped his face. "People have to buy into the sexy-actor-in-a-relationship sense, not the sexy-actor-hidden-under-a-jacket vibe."

"Does Kaden know we have to take our clothes off?" He couldn't help sounding pissed, but how was any of this necessary? Not that it stopped him from imagining Kaden in fewer clothes than a short-sleeved T-shirt. *Sue me, but he's hot.*

"Of course he knows."

"Are you sure this is the right thing to do? Shouldn't I be out there doing advocacy? Showing the general public I'm one of the good guys?"

She sighed then—the noise she made whenever he didn't *get* the point of celebrity—and he waited for the lecture.

"People will listen to your side when it's run on TMZ with a sexy photo of you and your exceptionally gorgeous boyfriend. They won't read an op-ed in the *New York Times*. You know this." She slid her hands to his shoulders, squeezed them, and then smoothed his T-shirt. "One night, Ryan. Then Arthur will release your press statement, and the two things will slot in nicely."

"Okay."

"Now, memorize the list, then give it back."

He wished he could take it with him, but the thought of the press getting hold of his meat run list was equally horrifying and hilarious. The paparazzi wanted certain things from their celebrities. No one bought the photo of the quiet dinner. They wanted the actress flashing her underwear taken through the back window of a limo or the actor being sick in the bushes and telling everyone to fuck off.

He ran through the list a few times, thanking the stars for his unique ability to remember his lines, which worked just as well for this list.

"I love you, Ry," Carmen called as he reached the door to leave. She sounded sad, and when he glanced back, his feisty sister had her arms wrapped around her and looked oddly vulnerable. She was his big sister and spent so many hours taking care of him, and he loved her more than anything in this world.

"I know, sis. I love you more."

She bit her lip. "You know, sometimes I wonder if it wouldn't be easier to tell everyone the truth."

Ryan dipped his head, and she must have caught the movement, because a brief flash of grief passed over her face. He hated that she'd seen him anything less than confident, and loathed that it was she who'd had to pick up the pieces of his mess. He'd put her through enough. "I can't do that."

Carmen's sympathetic gaze was sometimes unbearable. To tell anyone, beyond her and his therapist, the details of what had gone on with Paul and what he'd done to himself was terrifying.

Carmen backed down. "Good luck and text me."

He winked, pushing every ounce of sexy star into that one small thing. "I won't have time to text. I'll be having too much fun." He could lie just as well as the next guy.

"Whatever, loser."

That made him smile. He gave her the finger, and the last he saw was her cursing at him, but with a wide grin on her face.

It wasn't the same driver, and yet again, the question was asked whether the address was correct. Maybe tonight he'd ask Kaden where he lived and why he lived there, and if it was one of the penthouses in a business block, how the hell did he manage to afford it?

Of course, he couldn't precisely phrase it that way.

"Who am I kidding," he muttered and rolled his eyes at his self-delusion. "I'll say exactly that and end up looking like a fucking idiot."

"Sorry, Mr. Levesque?" He met the driver's gaze in the mirror and returned his polite smile.

"Nothing, I was just... practicing lines."

They were very close to Kaden's place now, and thankfully he didn't have to explain any more about who the hell he was calling a fucking idiot.

Kaden strode out again, just as sexy, just as confident, only this evening he was in dark jeans and a button-down, no jacket, and he waved for the driver to stay in the car and opened the door himself.

"Hey," Ryan said.

"Hey. You ready for this?"

"I was going to ask you the same thing."

Kaden counted off on his fingers, "Restaurant, two kisses, one handhold; at least I assume that is what HH is."

"It is," Ryan said with confidence. "I had to ask, though."

"Tin Lion Bar, hand on shoulder, talk, heads together, serious, then club, dance, shirts off, laugh a lot." He had the list down fine, but the expression on his face was comical.

"Have you done a meat run before?" Ryan asked.

"A what, now? Oh, is that what this is called? Then no, I haven't. I've done restaurants. And bars, and more than my fair share of VIP lounges in clubs, but all on the same night, no. You'll have to look after me."

His tone was teasing, and Ryan couldn't help the smile that formed. "I can try."

The restaurant was a well-known celebrity haunt, a sprawling sea of white tablecloths and crystal, and they were shown to a table right by the window. Kaden was one hundred percent gentleman, holding out Ryan's chair, pushing it in, then dropping a quick kiss to the top of Ryan's head. When he sat, he immediately took Ryan's hand and didn't release it as they checked the menu. They talked about the options, agreed to share a dessert after, and all through that, Ryan could imagine the cameras capturing everything.

Kaden rubbed circles with his thumb as they chatted about food, and it felt natural until the direction changed, and he ran a thumb over the inside of Ryan's wrist. Instinct screamed for Ryan to pull his hand back, but he didn't give in, pushing past the desperate desire to get the hell out of there before Kaden got too close and pretend-affectionate.

When the check arrived, Kaden took it smoothly, and Ryan didn't fight, because that wasn't the image they wanted to give. Kaden's back story was that of a wealthy businessman, and when they sealed the end of the meal with him sliding a card into the holder, followed by a soft kiss, it would look every inch a romantic gesture. The touch of Kaden's lips to his was electric, and he had to stop himself grabbing Kaden and tugging him closer.

"Another kiss down," Ryan murmured instead, and Kaden nodded.

"One kiss to go. Do you want to do that here? Or outside?"

Ryan considered the options. If he was a director, where would the kiss look best? Would it be here in the soft lighting or maybe out in the twilight on the street?

"Out," he half-whispered and wondered if he'd deliberately chosen that option to delay the inevitable and enjoy the anticipation because one small taste hadn't been enough.

Kissing Paul had been nothing like this, not even at the start when there had been an actual attraction, and Ryan couldn't recall the last time he'd gotten hard from kissing alone.

They held hands walking out of the restaurant, and then, when the door shut behind them, Ryan placed a hand on the back of Kaden's neck and held him, tilting his head and kissing him. The kiss was deep. There wasn't much room for breathing or thinking, and lust consumed Ryan in an instant. It had been so long since he'd been kissed properly. Even longer since he'd wanted to kiss back. He linked his hands at Kaden's neck and held on for the ride.

But it was the flare of a camera flash that had Kaden stepping away.

"Not here," he said, loud enough for anyone to hear who needed to. "It's too public, babe."

Kaden was good, doing this whole concerned lover thing very well. So well that Ryan had chased for more when they'd parted. Back in the car, they sat close, and Kaden added one more kiss that hadn't been on the list at all.

"Paparazzi out back," he explained.

"Good thinking," Ryan agreed, disappointed it hadn't been a kiss for the sake of it.

Kaden scooted away to the window, giving them some space. "I think that went well, so bar next."

"Uh-huh," Ryan said, still feeling the effects of the kissing and the accompanying lust that burned like wildfire inside. That kiss. That had been everything he'd ever wanted. The taste of it, the confidence, the experience—it was all the things that he'd never had with anyone else.

*I want more.*

*I can't have more. Not for real.*

In Tin Lion they seated at the bar, several people capturing them on their phones.

They bent their heads together.

"What should we talk about?" Ryan asked. "My sister suggested the price of sausages as a conversation starter."

Kaden huffed a laugh and placed his arm over Ryan's shoulder, leaning in and whispering in his ear. "Tell me why you became an actor."

Oh, well, that was an easy question.

"Carmen and I used to put on these plays when we

were little. I'd always be the hero of whatever drama we were doing. She'd be the heroine, the monster, the bad guy, the props manager, the director, and the one who fed me lines when I forgot. Sometimes she would do all of that in one show."

"You're obviously close to her."

"Very." Ryan tilted his beer and took a healthy swallow, then set it back down, flicking at the label with his thumbnail. "We had this house, with a wide hallway and a small balcony, and some of my best work was pretending to be Romeo up there. Or the prince who saves Rapunzel. I always wanted to act, I guess."

"School plays, that sort of thing?"

"Yep, I was mostly lead as I got older, great at remembering lines, so it was easy to choose me for the parts."

"Wouldn't have anything to do with being a good actor, then?" He was teasing, but Ryan bent his head a little lower, heat rising in his cheeks.

"Everyone who wants a part gets into a school play," he said with a shrug. The label was peeling away from the bottle now. "My first-ever part was in the school nativity."

"Joseph?"

"No, I was the apple."

Kaden laughed, "An apple? There's an apple in the nativity? Tell me more."

"Everyone knows there is an apple in the nativity, duh. I was six, and I had this awesome costume that my mom sewed, all by hand, that halfway through I could pull a cord, and it would change the outfit to look like someone had taken a bite from me."

Kaden was quiet, regarding him thoughtfully. "An

apple in a slice of apple pie America," he said. Ryan wanted to ask him what he meant, but the vibration in his watch told him they had to move on, and the club was so close they walked.

Ushered to the VIP area, they then drank a shot each, danced close, kissed a couple more times for effect, and when the next alarm went off, and it was time to go, Kaden unbuttoned his shirt and slipped it off. Ryan followed suit, and in thin T-shirts, they half ran out of the club, tripping over each other, getting the eager new lovers thing down perfectly.

At that moment they were paparazzi fodder, but Ryan had had one of the best nights of his life. Food, kisses, beer, more kisses, and now the quiet drive home with his head on Kaden's shoulder, where he'd rested as the car pulled away from the club. He hadn't moved away, and Ryan was sleepy, so there he stayed.

The car dropped Kaden off first.

"See you tomorrow for the whole beach house thing," he said.

The most significant part of this web of lies, where they'd be tested in front of the camera and interviews.

"Beach house for the hardest part."

"Nothing we can't handle."

"I guess." Ryan couldn't help sounding unsure because he was nervous. "Thank you for tonight."

Kaden quirked a smile. "It's what you pay me for."

"Yeah, I know. I didn't mean..." Shit, shit. Ryan changed the subject as Kaden unbuckled. "You know the articles about us with my statement on the video will run overnight."

"I know."

"If you have any questions..."

"Not right now. Night, Ryan."

*So that was it then. He's going.*

"Night," Kaden said firmly and walked away.

Ryan asked the driver to wait until Kaden had gone in through the door to the big glass building, and as soon as he had, they left.

*I wish he'd kissed me goodnight.*

## Chapter Five

*Freedom at last.* Kaden stepped out of the rental car onto the sandy driveway and filled his lungs with the ocean air. They'd flown out of JFK early that morning and followed up the six-hour flight with a fifty-minute drive to a private beach in Malibu. It was a little after ten in the morning, LA time.

He lifted his sunglasses, rested them on top of his head, and looked beyond the beach to the horizon. The water was calm and the view far grander than the one from his apartment. "It's beautiful."

"I prefer the mountains myself," Carmen said. She tucked her hair behind her ear. "Here." She tossed Kaden the keys. "How about you take Ryan inside and have a look around. I'll check on your luggage."

"Do you want a hand?"

"How gentlemanly of you." She patted his shoulder. "Thanks but no. Larry and I will bring it in." She inclined her head, indicating their driver.

"If you're sure." Kaden glanced at the key in his hand.

"You could have woken me." Ryan joined them outside the car. He squinted and shielded his eyes from the sunlight. "This the place?"

"Seems so," Kaden said.

Ryan had fallen asleep on the ride from the airport. Turning away from Kaden, he'd curled against the door and rested his head on his rolled-up sweater. His sleep had been peaceful, and the infrequent sounds of small puffed breaths had been a source of amusement for Kaden during the journey.

With a yawn, Ryan brushed his messy bangs out of his eyes, and Kaden couldn't help but smile.

Ryan met Kaden's gaze. "What?" Ryan rubbed at his shoulder.

"Nothing." Kaden chuckled. "I was just thinking about how bed hair suits you."

"My hair?" Ryan tried but failed to flatten the stray locks.

Carmen stepped forward. "Come here." She rubbed at his head.

"What are you doing?" Ryan jerked away. "You're so mean." He kept his distance, walking around her. "Mean," he said again, then grabbed Kaden's hand. "Let's go."

Ryan's grip was firm, his hand warm, and Kaden was caught off guard. In all their interactions so far, it had been Kaden who had taken the lead, instigated, improvised, so he was somewhat surprised to have Ryan initiate the contact.

"You okay?" Ryan asked when Kaden hesitated.

Kaden glanced at their hands. "Yes. Of course."

The house was situated at the end of the beach, nestled against a barrier of rocks, and there was enough distance between them and the next residence for privacy to not be an issue. Their accommodation was modern in appearance—stretches of glass and ninety-degree angles. It wasn't what Kaden had pictured when Ryan's people had said beach house. He'd had a more traditional image in his head. Weathered paint and wood panels. Something cozy, homey, yet whimsical.

Inside, Kaden slipped off his sneakers, sand sprinkling the shiny black tiles that covered the floor of the back half of the house. He breathed in. The house smelled of cleaning products and the sweet scent of some kind of air freshener. He scanned the open room. Kitchen and dining area at the back, then two steps led down to a large living area. Off to the side were three doors—bedrooms, bathroom, he figured.

"One thing I wouldn't miss if my career becomes a dumpster fire is all the traveling." Ryan stretched his arms above his head and let out a strained squeak as he stood on tiptoes.

Kaden had traveled many times as part of the job, albeit infrequently, both around the country and twice to Europe. "I can see how it might lose its appeal over time."

Ryan walked up to the floor-to-ceiling windows at the front of the house. "Do you like the beach?"

"I do." Kaden idled over to join Ryan. "Though it's the vast stretch of water that fascinates me the most."

"Can you swim?"

Kaden quirked an eyebrow. "Yes."

Ryan's eyes darted from side to side. "Too many rocks." He seemed disappointed. "Sorry. The studio picked this place."

"Rocks?" Kaden stared down at the beach.

"I'm not sure it's safe to swim."

Kaden shifted his attention to the crests of rocks visible above the water as waves rolled toward the shore. "Don't worry about it. I'm just happy I get to see the ocean again. It's been a while." He unlocked the sliding doors, which opened onto a decked area. He stepped outside, feeling the sun-warmed timber beneath his feet. "Honestly, I could stare at it all day."

At one side of the deck, shielded by a tall screen from the outside, was a Jacuzzi, in the center, a table and four chairs and two lounge chairs, and on the other side in front of what Kaden made out to be one of the bedrooms, was a covered area with a day bed hanging from the beams. He eyed the bed, a welcoming place of pillows and blankets that swung slightly in the warm breeze. The thought of wrapping himself up in the evening, watching the sun set into the ocean, left his heart aching for it to become a reality.

*Sounds nice.*

"I wonder if there's anyone else here." Ryan joined Kaden outside and followed him to the railing.

Kaden leaned back against the surround and glanced down the beach. "I'm pretty sure I saw a few cars parked outside the other places as we drove by."

"I guess a beach all to myself is a bit of a big ask."

"Maybe if you were top of that A-list thing I've heard about." Kaden tilted his head and smirked.

Ryan chuckled. "I'll get right on that." He folded his arms and rested them on the rail. "Eventually."

Kaden gave a small sigh. "Do you have your phone?"

"I think so." Ryan reached into the pocket of his sweater. "Why?"

Kaden slid his arms across the railing until his elbow bumped Ryan's. "We should take a picture." He took the phone from Ryan and opened the camera app. Kaden held his arm out as far as he could and leaned in close to Ryan, who looked back at the camera from over his shoulder.

"Say beach," Kaden said cheerfully and gave a wide smile.

Ryan's face brightened, his gaze settling on Kaden. "Beach," he said.

Kaden took the photo. "There you go." He handed the phone back to Ryan. "For Instagram or whatever."

"Thanks."

"We should take some more when we can. Different places, different outfits, maybe some obscure couple-type images. That way, once the contract ends, you can still post them for a while." Their "relationship" would continue beyond the end of the week and the red carpet premiere. Ryan was to drop occasional reminders and photos of them on social media, and in the space of a few weeks or a couple of months, the mentions would become fewer and fewer until Kaden disappeared from his life, their fleeting romance having fizzled to nothing. A mutual separation.

"'Couple-type' pictures?" Ryan raised an eyebrow.

"You know, like a photo of our hands doing that heart thing, you in one of my sweaters, our feet sticking out from under a blanket together, a drink with two straws, a dessert with two spoons. Things that imply romance." Kaden shrugged. "The Levesquers would love that kind of thing, right?"

Ryan laughed. "You know the name of my fanbase?"

"Someone at the office mentioned it." After his dates with Ryan, Kaden had debriefed with Rowan. Levesquers had come up when Rowan had tried to convince Kaden he wasn't some super fan despite sounding like the writer of Ryan's Wiki page for the majority of the meeting.

"I see." Ryan almost looked disappointed.

"If you're doing anything inappropriate, cut it out. We're coming in," Carmen called, though she was already inside.

Ryan cleared his throat and stood straight. He glanced at Kaden, then lowered his gaze to the deck floor. "Coming," he shouted back.

For a moment, Kaden closed his eyes, listened to the water's movements. He was filled with a sense of peace.

*I should probably make the most of it.*

He didn't know the full list of items on the agenda for the week, but what he had seen involved people. Lots of people.

When he opened his eyes, his gaze settled on the space beside him. Maybe there were some views better shared with others. Pushing off the rail, he took a deep breath before following Ryan inside.

"The master bedroom is at the front." Carmen locked her gaze on Kaden as he stepped through the door. "The second bedroom is for your use, and that's at the back." She dragged a suitcase over to the L-shaped sofa. "But there'll be people all over this house the next few days, so don't go making it too obvious."

Kaden gave a brief salute. "Yes, ma'am."

Carmen stopped in her tracks and smirked. "I'll give you fifteen minutes to settle in. Then we'll go over the itinerary for the rest of the week."

"How generous of you, sis." Ryan knelt on the couch and draped his arms over the back. "Do we really have to go for drinks tonight?" He quirked his head and gave her doe eyes. "I'd rather spend a night in with my *boyfriend*. Watch the sunset as we sip beer in the hot tub."

"Cute." She glanced over her shoulder as Larry entered with a large carry-on and another case. "I know you don't want to go, but you need to show your face. Imelda, Jackson and Kayleigh are handling the talk shows, so you need to be visible when you can."

Ryan rested his chin on the sofa and glanced up at her. "I know."

"Who knows what new opportunities might come from it."

"I know," he said again.

"Head up, remember. You've got to show them that fighting spirit." She raised her fists. "Just no actual fighting. I don't need that headache." With a sigh, she looked at Kaden. "I can trust you to keep him out of trouble, can't I?"

"He'll be fine." Kaden sat on the couch.

"I'll be fine," Ryan said straight after.

Carmen folded her arms. "See that you are. Right, we'll get the last of your things. I might head over to the hotel and get Larry and me checked in. We can talk about the week's plans when I get back."

"Okay." Ryan lifted his head.

"Only thing you need to know right now is the studio has arranged a car for you to the Merrington tonight, so it won't be Larry. It will get here around seven, so be ready." She frowned in thought. "There should be arrangements to get you back, but any problems contact me."

"What are you doing tonight?"

"Larry doesn't know it yet, but he's treating *me* to drinks at our hotel bar." She leaned her head when Larry stopped beside her. He wore a despairing expression. "And then I might take a long soak in the tub with a good book." Larry continued toward the door, and Carmen followed. "We'll be back for lunch, so you're free to do as you please until then. Unpack, explore, take a nap. We'll see you later."

Ryan waved. "Okay. See ya."

And then they were alone. Kaden considered his options.

*A nap sounds good.*

"Are you okay if I try and grab an hour or two?" He nodded toward the bedroom door.

Ryan ran his hand under his jaw. "Sure."

"Is that okay? If you want some company, I don't mind staying out here."

Ryan shook his head. "No. Really, I'm fine." He stretched his arms out in front of him. "Get some sleep. I can entertain myself. Unpack or something."

Kaden stood. "If you're sure." He yawned and picked up one of the bags that'd been brought in. "I'll put most of my stuff in with yours if that's okay. For appearance's sake."

He wasn't sure how many people would be walking through the beach house in the coming days. There was tomorrow's photoshoot, an exclusive behind-closed-doors type interview for one magazine, as well as two days of promotional interviews for the movie, though as he recalled, the second day involved at least one other cast member and was being held elsewhere. There were also some additional events to attend, including tonight's drinks at the Merrington Hotel.

"Thanks," Ryan said and smiled. "I really mean it."

Kaden nodded and hoisted the bag's strap higher on his shoulder. "You know where I am if you need me." He took a single step toward the bedroom. "Oh, and feel free to come take a cute picture of your sleeping boyfriend. You know, for the Levesquers." He chuckled and carried on to his room. "Later, Ryan."

"Yeah, later."

The rest of the day flew by in a regimented blur, and before Kaden knew it, the car for the hotel sounded its horn, and they were heading out the door.

"How many of these people do you actually know?" Kaden asked as he leaned close to Ryan, who smelled delicious. They were standing in the large reception room of the Merrington Hotel, surrounded by people Kaden didn't know.

"A couple of dozen at most." Ryan pressed his hand to Kaden's chest. "It'll be over soon. We can start saying our good-byes and head for the reception, get them to arrange a car back."

Kaden smiled, then pressed a kiss to Ryan's cheek. It had been another night of faked smiles and conversation. He'd almost been glad to see Imelda earlier, a friendly face among a sea of strangers, but she'd long gone on a tour of the room.

"Ryan. I thought that was you. How are you?"

Kaden stepped back and checked out the man beside them. His appearance was unassuming, another suit in a room of suits.

"Why are you at a closed party?" Ryan shifted his footing, straightened his back, and his voice was low but accusing.

The man fiddled with the cuffs of his shirt. "Here? Dad's company represents one of the investors for your little movie. He was invited, but you know how he is. So he sent me in his stead." The man turned his gaze to Kaden. "And who is this? I don't believe we've met."

Kaden glanced from the man to Ryan. *What is this?* Ryan struggled to raise his head, his complexion paling as he curled his fingers into the material of Kaden's jacket. Kaden held out his hand. "I'm—"

"This is my boyfriend, Kaden," Ryan blurted out. He lifted his head. "Kaden, this is Paul." He put his hand on Kaden's arm.

*Paul.* Kaden looked at his hand as Paul took hold of it. His shake was aggressive, his grip too tight.

"Paul Feldstone. You might recognize the name from my father's law firm." Paul pulled his arm back.

Kaden turned his hand and stared at his palm. *Paul.* Guilt crept through him for not realizing it straight away, but he had only heard the name once. Ryan's past relationship wasn't a topic either of them wanted to bring up again. This was Paul. *That* Paul. The one from the past and the subject of Ryan's video rant? He glanced at Ryan, who stood tall at his side. Kaden didn't really understand where the feeling came from, but he was proud of Ryan at that moment.

"I'm sorry. Feldstone doesn't sound familiar," he said.

*What should I do?* Kaden rested his hand over Ryan's and squeezed it, and from the darkening of Paul's gaze, the offer of comfort hadn't gone unnoticed.

Disgust for the man in front of him tightened Kaden's chest. He didn't know the full story, hadn't asked. That wasn't the role he'd been paid to take on. It wasn't his place. All he could do was let Ryan know he wasn't alone.

With a smile on his face, Kaden leaned in close and pressed a light kiss to Ryan's cheek.

"Too much champagne, babe?" he said and rubbed Ryan's hand. It was hard to ignore Ryan's sullen features. Paul would be well aware of them too.

Ryan met his eyes. "Maybe." He cleared his throat as he searched Kaden's gaze.

Kaden smiled, hoping his eyes conveyed what he wanted to say out loud.

*And I'm right here with you.*

# Chapter Six

Ryan gripped Kaden's hand.

Hard.

But Kaden didn't pull away or say a single word after pretending in an obvious way to Paul that they were in a relationship.

Paul's expression hardened, even though he was smiling. "So, Ry, how have you been? I imagine things must have been quite hard for you these last few weeks."

"They have," Kaden answered before Ryan had a chance to say anything. "But he's..." He turned, met Ryan's eyes, and they held such warmth. He leaned in for another kiss. "He's been amazing." Kaden looked back at Ryan. "I'm proud to be at his side."

Paul's focus was on where Ryan's arm was linked with Kaden's. "Did you get any of my messages?" His gaze was cold as steel and just as weighty. "I was worried when you didn't reply. I know how you've let things get you down in the past."

*The past.* Ryan's chest stung with the emotion.

Paul reached out, rested his hand on Ryan's shoulder. "You have my support if you need it."

Ryan lowered his shoulder, breaking the contact with Paul's hand. "Thank you," he managed. The words felt like poison on his lips. "I've been busy. It must have slipped my mind." The swell in his chest was making him want to scream, but this was not the time or place to make a scene.

"Have you two known each other long?" Kaden asked all of a sudden.

"We're old friends," Paul said. "Though we no longer get to see each other as much as I'd like." His voice sliced through Ryan, his words loaded with the history between them. "It'd be great to catch up properly some time."

"We'd love that, wouldn't we, babe?" Kaden squeezed Ryan's waist, hugging him close as if to claim him. "Maybe you could contact Carmen and have her arrange something. It'll probably have to be *way* in the future. I mean, Ryan's schedule is so hectic at the moment. I'm so incredibly lucky he brought me with him this week." Kaden honestly sounded excited and part of Ryan's life. "I never knew how much time went into the buildup to a movie release. I can't believe I'll be with him on premiere night. *My* Ryan and I on the red carpet."

"Without my firm's support of one of your key investors, I doubt this film would have happened at all." There was a bitter edge to Paul's tone.

*Ah, there it is—a crack in his charming form.*

"I'm sorry," Kaden said with a tone that suggested he wasn't sorry at all and so different from only moments ago. "I thought you just said it was your father's firm. I must have misunderstood." Paul bristled, and there was a familiar flash of cruelty in his eyes.

Ryan's heart beat faster. What was this? Though he appreciated Kaden coming to his defense, was Kaden trying to push Paul to a reaction? That never ended well, and Kaden had to understand the type of man he was dealing with.

Paul straightened, shoulders back, and narrowed his gaze.

*I want to run. I need to go.*

Jeez, these were two alpha males confronting each other, and this was the last thing Ryan wanted. The thought of Paul messing with his head and then moving onto Kaden was like burning acid inside him.

"Mr. Feldstone?" A man appeared at Paul's side. He narrowed his eyes as he noticed Ryan, and next to Kaden, Ryan stiffened.

"Luke," Ryan murmured. "It's been a while."

"Ryan," Luke replied.

"How are you?"

Luke shook his head, then pressed a hand to Paul's arm. "Sorry to interrupt, but Mr. Barrett's asking for you."

"Who?" Paul switched his weight onto his other foot.

"The gentleman your father mentioned."

"Oh, yes. Barrett." Paul glanced at Ryan. "I need to deal with this, but it was nice seeing you." He stepped closer. "Think about what I told you in my messages." He straightened, his gaze shifting to Kaden. "Have a good evening," he said. He turned, knocking Luke's shoulder as he passed. "Luke, with me."

Luke didn't say anything, briefly locking eyes with Ryan before following Paul.

"Are you okay?" Kaden pressed his hand to Ryan's back.

"Get off me." Ryan put space between them. *What is this feeling? I thought I'd gotten stronger. But no, one minute in his presence and I'm ready to run.* "I'm going to the bathroom."

"Do you want me to come with you?" Kaden's brow creased.

Ryan shook his head. "Stay here. Or better yet, go and check on our ride home. I want to go back."

"Okay. I can do that."

*I need space.*

Ryan eased himself through the crowds. Was Paul among them? He kept his head low, avoided looking at faces. His thoughts went to Luke. He was Paul's PA? Or what? Luke must know what an asshole Paul was. Why was he here?

He felt lightheaded and filled his lungs as he stepped into the bathroom. He headed for the sinks, gripping the edge of the marble counter as he rocked forward. His mouth was dry, and he found it hard to swallow and clear his throat. *Somehow*, although his entire life had shifted in an instant, and he wanted to slide to the floor, curl in on himself, Ryan managed to stay on his feet. He'd known that Feldstone's was working with the investors, and even though he had voiced his fears of seeing Paul, in reality, there were several steps between him and Paul, so this shouldn't have happened.

*But it did.* Reality wasn't on his side.

"It's okay," he whispered to his reflection. "It's done now."

When the bathroom door opened, Ryan lifted his head to see Luke.

Luke didn't say anything at first, instead walked the

line of stalls, pushing each one and ensuring they were empty. Finally, he came to stand in front of Ryan.

"Hi, Luke," Ryan said and straightened his back. He wasn't expecting a hug or anything. After everything that had happened, he and Luke had drifted apart.

"Hi? Sure, Ryan." Luke folded his arms across his chest. "So I'm going to need you to stay away from Paul."

Ryan widened his eyes. "What?"

"I don't want you ruining everything all over again."

*What the hell is going on here?* Ryan felt sick.

"Paul doesn't need you in his life. He has me now," he said as he glared at Ryan.

"You?" Ryan leaned against the counter. "You're with him? Why would you do that? You know what he's like; you saw it all."

"He's good to me. What we have is different from what you had."

"I want to be happy for you, Luke, but a leopard never changes his spots. Is he hurting you?"

Luke tilted his chin. "I'm not a child like you were, always pushing him. We have an adult relationship."

"And he came out to his family for you?" Ryan knew the answer, even as he asked the question.

Luke huffed. "You know as well as I do the position he's in with his father. He can't just come out and tell them about our relationship. He's not like you, spreading everything you feel all over social media."

"So, that's a no." Ryan shook his head. "Why do you think I'd want anything to do with Paul?"

Luke stepped closer. "I know he contacted you. He felt bad for you, even though that video was aimed at him. I can't believe you would release something like that as propaganda for a damn movie. No wonder he was never faithful to you when you were together if you had this much hate inside you."

Ryan narrowed his eyes. He knew there had been other men, that he hadn't been good enough to satisfy Paul. After all, Paul had told him so. A bad boyfriend, bad at love, bad at sex. Must try harder. But Luke was talking as if he was excusing Paul. "You have no idea what you're talking about."

"Really? Who do you think he came to for comfort? Who do you think supported him? He told me all about how messed up you were back then. Do you know how hard it is for him to have a normal healthy relationship with someone now?"

*What fresh hell is this?*

"Luke, I don't know what he's been saying, but I can't do this right now."

*I need to get out of here.*

Luke stepped into his path. "You might have broken him, but I'll be the one to fix him when he has his bad times. I love him, and if you ever loved him, then you'll leave him alone."

"Me leave him alone?"

*I'm in hell.*

"I can make him happy." Luke's tone turned desperate; his eyes held a plea. "I try really hard, so just stay away."

Ryan's chest tightened. Behind the bluster, there was a vulnerability, and he had a sudden flash of empathy for his old friend.

"Look, Luke, you don't have to stay with him," Ryan said urgently. He pulled out his cell. "Take my number, and if you need my help—"

"I love him," Luke sounded defiant, but he couldn't quite meet Ryan's gaze.

*This could be me, standing here and trying to tell myself that I was happy.*

"Luke, is he—?"

"I've said everything I need to." The bathroom door opened. Luke glanced over his shoulder as a man entered and headed into one of the stalls. Luke stepped back toward the door. "Please. Leave us alone," he said, then left.

Ryan gripped the counter. Frustration twisted inside him. His head was a mess. Anger. Fear. Guilt.

*Fuck.*

He took some deep breaths, tried to calm himself down. He needed to make it to reception and out to the car, and he pasted on a smile. Was it convincing enough? It would have to do.

Back in the car, Ryan curled in the corner defensively.

"You can't do that with Paul. You can't goad him into reacting," he snapped. God knows how Paul would take his frustrations out on Luke. Anger and compassion and fear, all boiled inside him, but he'd kept it together long enough to pose for a few photos, even signed a couple of autographs. In the car, however, with the privacy screen and blacked-out windows, all bets were off. He hadn't been able to shake the mixed-up nightmare inside his head. He was angry. Scared. Confused.

"I wanted him to know we're together; that is the point, right?" Kaden talked as if he hadn't poked the hornet's nest.

"I know that, but what about the rest of it? You can't

act as though you have something over him—he'll take that as a challenge," Ryan said, the acid in his belly making him feel sick, lightheaded and about ready to be out in the fresh air. Part of him had expected the worst to happen. Every single time he stepped out of the house, he thought about what he'd do if he saw Paul again, heightened with this entire mess. Abruptly his guard was up. How could he trust Kaden—he didn't even know him?

"I wasn't challenging him, Ryan."

"Don't patronize me, and yes, you were. You didn't have to say anything to him. We could have walked away, and he would have left us alone, but now he'll be angry, and Luke…" *Why did you say anything at all to him?*

"I wasn't being condescending, and I apologize if I misunderstood my role." Kaden shrugged as he said it, and all Ryan thought was that he didn't mean a word of what he said.

"Fuck you."

"Ryan—"

"I don't pay you to make a mess of things."

As soon as the words left his mouth, he wished he could pull them back. He was angry, but Kaden wasn't the only one at fault. He blamed Paul, and he blamed himself, and most of all, he feared for Luke. What was he doing? It was too easy to take this whole mess out on Kaden. He was right there next to him. *I'm paying him. I'm in control.* For a few moments, Ryan felt that was true until Kaden held out a hand as a sign of peace.

"I'm sorry," Kaden murmured, and that was too much.

"I don't need you to keep apologizing if you don't

mean it. I need you to shut the hell up." Ryan took a shaky breath.

Kaden nodded, and they slipped into an uncomfortable silence. When they, at last, reached the beach house, Ryan clambered out of the car, desperate for air. The call of the ocean was enough for him to change direction from heading inside where he might have had to talk to a confused-looking Kaden. He scrambled over the rocks in the dark, tripping and falling, and reaching the sand, took off his shoes and headed for the obsidian water. He heard Kaden struggling to follow and moved farther into the water, the waves lapping up past his ankles, soaking his pants.

Kaden caught up with him, tugging at his jacket and holding tight. "Don't go far; stay there." He sounded a little panicked.

"What do you think I'm going to do? Walk into the damn ocean?"

"How the hell would I know what you're going to do?" Kaden asked.

Ryan shook off his hold and stepped back, stumbling as his feet sunk into the sand, a particularly big wave breaking around him, and he righted himself, holding out his hands in protection as Kaden reached for him.

"I'm not him." Kaden raised his voice over the noise of the breaking waves, but he didn't move closer. "I won't hurt you."

"Leave me alone, okay!"

Kaden shook his head. "I'm not leaving you out here alone."

Ryan took a few more steps away. Then it hit him that Kaden meant what he'd said—there was no way he was going to get peace here right now. He left, taking it more carefully, moving back to the house, and then he sat on the swing on the wide porch, in the dark, staring out at the ocean. Kaden followed him back but went inside. No doubt, he was still watching Ryan.

"You're not my bodyguard," he muttered and pushed the swinging bed into a slow rocking motion, temper and fear tight inside him. He thought he'd have been stronger the next time he met Paul, but he'd been the same scared kid who'd let himself be pushed around. He pulled out his cell, wiped the damp off the screen, and thumbed through his contacts to his sister.

"Hey," she said on a yawn.

"Sorry, did I wake you up?"

"Uh-huh, and I was dreaming I was getting hot and heavy with Chris Hemsworth. This'd better be good."

Ryan wanted to be able to tease her about the fact that she was having dreams featuring his favorite Chris. He was desperate to be in a good place that meant he could tease her and not be feeling the rug had been yanked from under him.

"Paul was at the party."

She went silent, and he heard her moving, imagining her getting out of bed, pulling on her robe, and knowing he'd wrecked her sleep for maybe the rest of the night. She'd been the one to help him through everything that had happened, been his rock, and when she'd found him that fateful morning, she'd made him promise always to tell her everything.

"Shit," she said with feeling. "What did he say to you? What happened? Talk to me."

*I want to. But I don't want to.* He wanted to forget about Paul, about Luke, about the whole damn evening.

"He was with Luke. Remember him?"

"Luke Hart? The kid you used to hang around with?"

"Yeah, and Luke and Paul are an item, and I see the same fear in Luke that I used to have." *That I still have.* "And Kaden made everything awful." It felt good to divert attention from himself onto Kaden. One more thing to feel bad about later. How did Ryan explain the way Kaden confronted Paul, about the helplessness that knifed through Ryan seeing the two men face off? Kaden wasn't anything like Paul, but he'd also pushed at Paul, and that wasn't going to end well.

"I didn't feel safe," Ryan admitted. That was what she'd made him promise to say if he ever felt as if things were out of control. The day she'd found him with the blades and the blood and crying, that had been the moment she'd taken control over it all. Without her, he'd have been lost, and only with her had he managed the counseling and had come out the other side a stronger person. He'd been convinced that he'd be able to handle Paul if he ever crossed his path. And now? Two minutes maximum in his company and he was losing that control he'd fought so hard to cultivate.

"Do we need to call the police?" she asked urgently.

"And tell them what exactly? That I saw someone who is completely out of my life? That he's clearly with someone who doesn't know any better. We knew this could happen out here. I just thought I'd be more prepared, and at first, I was okay. Then it all got fucked up when Kaden…"

"What about Kaden? Talk to me."

What was he supposed to say? Kaden had been doing exactly what he'd been paid for. "He acted like a boyfriend."

"What?"

"He wasn't doing it on purpose, really, but he might have been a bit too convincing. Paul reacted badly."

"Maybe we should have explained to Kaden about Paul and what—"

"The damage is done," Ryan interrupted. There was no point in talking about what they should have done. He'd compartmentalized Paul's shit, and he hadn't wanted to share it, least of all with a boyfriend he'd hired.

"I'm coming over right now."

"No, I don't need you to do that. Kaden played his part well. It was just a shock to see Paul after all this time."

And then there was Luke. Was he really in a relationship with Paul? The look on his face as he'd as good as begged Ryan to stay away was scarily familiar. He was sure it was an expression Carmen would have recognized, one he'd worn as he insisted what went on between him and Paul was none of her business. How blinded he'd been back then. And now he felt wrong, as if not voicing his concerns and making what had happened to him public meant that young guys like Luke would get sucked into Paul's orbit.

*I need to talk to Luke. I need to do something. We used to be friends. There's no reason we couldn't be again.*

"Are you sure? I can be there in ten."

Ryan cleared his throat and pulled his concentration back to his sister. "I'm sure. Love you."

"I love you back, but don't change the subject. Are you going to be okay?"

"I promise I am."

Hearing her voice had calmed him down enough to

at least attempt to process what had happened that evening.

They ended the call, and for a little while, Ryan sat listening to the ocean and trying not to think about anything at all.

"That was stupid of me," Kaden said from the doorway, the soft light from inside the house spilling out around him. "There was something about Paul I didn't like. I misunderstood, and I'm not here to cause trouble. I'm here to be your partner."

Ryan scrubbed at his eyes. "You didn't know. I overreacted, lost control. I should be the one to apologize."

Kaden sat next to him on the swing, the warmth of him welcome against the cold of his wet-through pants.

"In my defense, I was living the whole protective boyfriend thing. I don't normally go around stamping my possession on my partners."

"I tell myself you were acting, but it was all so real." Ryan winced at how needy he sounded and hated that the sensory trigger of seeing Paul was undoing years of counseling in an instant. All the negative habits he'd slipped into after Paul were forcing their way to the surface: the panic, the lashing out at the nearest person. It was all there.

"I'm not him," Kaden interrupted his spiral of shame.

Ryan could let this go, not begin to explain, but there were a few tools in his arsenal his counselor had taught him, short explanations that meant he didn't have to go too deep into his memories.

"I know that," he lied because even with Carmen's vetting and the contracts in place, who really knew a man until they lived with him for a while? Paul had changed from being the confident older guy to someone controlling, slowly and so subtly Ryan hadn't even noticed at first. "This is all confidential, like a doctor-patient thing, and if you give any interviews, then under the terms of our contract, I have the right to sue you and your company for every cent you have. And believe me, I will do that at the drop of a hat."

He looked at Kaden then, facing him head-on, waiting for Kaden's anger. There was only compassion and understanding. Kaden wasn't acting like Paul. He gave the impression of being a different kind of man, and for a brief moment, Ryan wanted to do more than fake-kiss him.

The contract included PDAs in public, but there was no one here to see them kiss, so he couldn't even ask Kaden for a hug. After all, he was the one who threatened to sue if contracts were broken.

"I know how to keep confidences. And I understand how hard it is to trust after being so badly burned in the past," Kaden said.

"You do?"

"I do." He didn't expand on the statement and held out a hand to shake, which Ryan took. At the last moment, Kaden turned over Ryan's hand and pressed a kiss to the palm before releasing his hold. "And maybe that's something we both need to work on, but right now, we need to go over tomorrow's itinerary. Then you should try and get some sleep."

The kiss was shockingly erotic for such a gentle touch, and heat flooded Ryan. Intimacy was something he avoided to keep himself safe, but that simple kiss sparked something in him that was a lot like confusion.

Kaden stood and Ryan stared up at him thoughtfully. Ryan struggled with trust, and it seemed he wasn't the only one. Old memories and new feelings were tangling inside him.

Sleep would be a long time coming.

## Chapter Seven

"Good morning," Carmen shouted as she threw the drapes open.

When light flooded the living room, Kaden winced and raised his hand to shield his eyes. "Too loud," he uttered. "And way too bright."

Carmen turned and folded her arms across her chest. She looked down at him with a curious expression. "Last night's clothes, huh? You remember you have your own bed, right?"

Kaden sat up and rubbed his face. "Yes. I remember." Though he had managed to take a nap in there yesterday, the space unnerved him, triggered old traumas. The room was dimly lit, cramped, too small for the twin single beds and large dresser. The mirrored sliding doors of the closet did little for the illusion of space. In fact, they made Kaden feel more closed in as he was faced with the reflection of himself and the blank, solid wall behind him.

With a sigh, Carmen glanced toward Ryan's closed bedroom door. "I heard about your run-in with he-who-is-an-asshole last night. Paul has a habit of upsetting the balance."

"I see that now." He slipped into a brief silence and stared at the floor. "I messed up." He breathed in and met her eyes. "But I guess you already know that." Ryan had been on the phone with her last night, leaving Kaden feeling useless. There was nothing he could have done to offer Ryan comfort, not in the way Carmen could.

"You did." She pursed her lips. "But then it wasn't as if you had all the facts at the time."

"Pretty sure I still don't." He shook his head. Morning weariness hung in his voice. "I didn't mean... I don't expect Ryan or you to tell me everything about an obviously private matter. Just that—"

"It might have helped? Want me to make you a presentation? Maybe a nice flowchart, all color-coded and stuff?" Her tone was light, with a hint of nervous humor.

*Guess she doesn't blame me for last night.* "A graph of assholery for that guy might be useful."

"Sure. I'll run it past Ryan and see what I can do." She rested her hands on her hips. "Now feel free not to answer, but why were you sleeping out here?"

Kaden blinked and glanced beyond Carmen to the beach. He considered being honest. To tell her how stifled he'd felt in the small second bedroom. How he felt obliged to shut the door, close himself off, despite the tense feeling that swelled in his chest when he did. *Should I?* He wasn't in the mood if Carmen chose to pry further into his private life. Would she even understand?

After his father had walked out on his mom, Kaden had lived his life in a state of constant fear. Not genuine fear, but the unpredictability of his mother's mood made him wary of every word he spoke, every action he took. A misstep and in an instant her temper would flare, and everything wrong in her life was his fault. There were times she would scream and shout, times she would pull his hair, and then there was the windowless storage room, the bolt on its door, where she left him behind alone and in darkness.

*Yeah, not talking about that.*

"No particular reason." He stretched his arms above his head. "Stayed up late. Fell asleep out here." He flashed her a smile as she narrowed her eyes.

"Uh-huh."

There was a *click* of a door, and Ryan emerged from his room. "What are you doing?" He squinted as he looked between them and the window. With a yawn, he wandered barefoot to the sofa and curled himself up in the corner. The knee-length shorts he was wearing rolled up his thighs as he raised his knees to his chest. "You're so loud, sis. What time is it?"

"Six-thirty," Carmen stated.

Ryan yawned again and pushed up his hooded sweater to scratch his stomach.

Kaden's gaze was briefly drawn to Ryan's navel and the small roll of flesh at his stomach due to the way he was sitting, hugging the corner of the couch. He looked away when Ryan settled his eyes on him. Did he have something to say about last night?

Ryan didn't speak to him. Instead, he asked Carmen, "What do you need me to do?"

Carmen checked him out. "First, you can grab yourself a shower." She then turned to Kaden. "You too," she said in a firm tone.

*What did I do?* Kaden sat up straight, and Ryan chuckled.

"Then we're going to sit down, eat breakfast, and have a little chat."

"A chat?" Kaden furrowed his brow.

"Clear the air, talk about your feelings, hug it out. I don't care, so long as you get your heads back in the game called *faking it* before the crew for the magazine shows up."

Clear the air? *How am I supposed to do that?* Kaden had no idea what he was supposed to say or how to say it.

It was Ryan who broke the stalemate. "Sorry." Ryan gazed out the window. He rested his chin on the heel of his hand. "Sorry if I overreacted." His voice was muffled as he spoke through his curled fingers.

To Kaden, it appeared as if Carmen was going to press Ryan further, but it wasn't Ryan's fault things had gotten weird last night. Well, maybe a little, but Kaden had overstepped. "And I'm sorry if my behavior upset you. It was never my intention."

Carmen clapped her hands together. "So we're all good?" she checked.

"Yes, we're good," Ryan said. His body relaxed, and he faced Kaden. "We're not hugging, though." A smile teased the corner of his mouth, and his face brightened.

Kaden chuckled. "I can live with that."

Ryan lowered his legs and slid to the edge of the cushion. "How long before people start showing up?"

After checking her phone, Carmen said, "Ninety minutes."

"Okay." He got to his feet but hesitated in front of Kaden. "We are okay, aren't we?" He met Kaden's eyes.

*What is he thinking?*

Kaden nodded. "Of course." He still had a job to do, and he intended on doing it.

"Thanks." Ryan took a deep breath, steeling himself for the day ahead. "Right. Okay. Shower."

Carmen watched Ryan as he headed back to his room. She wore a serious expression and lifted her glasses to rub her eyes.

"You're still worried about him?" Kaden said.

"Who? Me?" Carmen folded her arms. "He'll be fine. He's stronger than he looks. Besides, he's got me." She glanced at Kaden and pursed her lips. "And you for the time being." For a moment, she fell silent. "I can't speak for Ryan, but I want you to know I trust you… with him."

*She trusts me?* Kaden ran his knuckles over his chest. Her trust was a weight he hadn't been prepared for. *How can she give it so easily?* It wasn't something he was quick to give, and he could probably count the people he trusted on one hand.

Carmen said, "It's going to be a long day. Are you ready?" She encouraged him with a smile.

Kaden gazed out the window at the clear blue sky. "Yeah. I'm ready."


"We're going to break for lunch."

The announcement stirred Kaden from the book he'd been reading, his gaze drawn to one of the assistants he'd briefly been introduced to jogging across the sand. With a sigh, he slipped a bookmark between the pages and closed the paperback. Placing it on the day bed beside him, he sat forward. The bed swayed as he moved. He picked up one of the cushions and hugged it to his chest, scanning the beach for Ryan.

*There you are.*

Ryan sat cross-legged on a towel in the shadow of a large umbrella, wearing a pair of headphones. His head was down, his attention on his phone.

"Kaden," Carmen said, tapping the window as she spoke to make sure she had his attention. "Here." She held out a wrapped sub roll and smiled. "Thought you might want to give it to him."

"Is he doing okay?" Kaden took the sandwich. He had watched Ryan on a few occasions during the morning. He didn't understand the business, didn't want to, but Ryan seemed to be handling the shoot and the people around him.

"Seems to be. I think it's better for him when he's busy."

Busy could be good. Kaden glanced over at Ryan, then checked around them. It was just him and Carmen. "Anything I should do in particular? Nothing has been specified about today other than hanging out in the background and casting a few adoring looks his way throughout the day."

Carmen shook her head. "I'm sure you'll make it look convincing, whatever you do." She leaned against the window. "So, off you go."

"Right." Kaden left the swing bed and, with the sandwich, made his way down to the beach. He stopped for a moment as his feet sank into the warm golden sand. He made his way to where Ryan was sitting and crouched beside him in the shaded area. Ryan didn't notice him at first, and Kaden spent a long moment observing him. His long bangs had been styled to one side, and he could see the faint shimmer of makeup across his skin. There was a low hum of music, but nothing Kaden could make out.

"What…" Ryan flinched and pushed the headphones back off his ears. "Where did you come from?" He fumbled with his phone, swiping at the screen, stopping the music. He rested his phone face down in his lap.

"Didn't mean to scare you."

Ryan cleared his throat, glancing at his phone. "You didn't." He shuffled sideways, making room for Kaden to drop forward to kneel beside him on the towel. "Did Carmen send you?"

"In part." Kaden held out the sandwich. He set his mouth at an angle as he eyed Ryan's phone. Why did he feel as if Ryan wasn't telling him something? No, he shouldn't pry. Not after what had happened last night. "To be honest, I could do with the company."

Ryan took the food. "Sorry. You must be bored out of your mind."

"I'll survive." Kaden sat and stared out at the ocean. "Plus I'm learning new things. I mean, turns out there's a lot more to this stuff than one man with a camera."

He had been surprised by how many people were milling around the beach and house. Staff from a variety of departments doing a multitude of things— hair, makeup, wardrobe, catering, lighting, framing; several assistants.

"I'm just relieved the magazine didn't pull the whole thing when news of the video hit," Ryan said, though his words didn't match his expression. Was he really relieved?

Kaden glanced behind them. He could imagine

what Ryan was thinking, how he'd assume everyone was talking about him behind his back. Maybe some people were. "They must have faith in you."

"You mean faith the outrage will have blown over by the time the magazine hits the stands next month."

Kaden didn't know what to say. Instead, he leaned to the side until his shoulder touched Ryan's. He focused on the sound of the waves lapping the shore. The voices faded, and a sense of peace fell over him. He smiled as Ryan unwrapped his lunch.

"Did you already eat?" Ryan asked.

Kaden shook his head. "I'll find something later. I'll have time to kill once you get back to work." He pressed his hand to his stomach, hoping it wouldn't betray him.

"Here." Ryan tore the roll in two. He offered Kaden the smaller of the pieces. "For you."

Kaden raised a hand. "Thanks, but I'm fine."

"I'm not that hungry. So we can share."

"Really, you should eat it. Keep your energy up for the afternoon session."

Ryan gave a noisy sigh. "Just take the damn sandwich." He pushed it into Kaden's hand.

Kaden looked at the partly flattened roll. "Okay. Okay. I give up." He turned the sandwich over, eyeing the salad that spilled out of the sides. "Thank you," he said, noting how Ryan relaxed his shoulders and the corners of his mouth twitched.

They sat together quietly and ate. When they had finished, Kaden took Ryan's hand in his. He laced his fingers with Ryan's. "I think I'm in love."

Ryan's grip tightened. "Love?"

"Yeah. With this view."

Ryan laughed and backhanded Kaden's shoulder.

"What was that for?"

"You scared me for a minute."

Kaden stretched out his legs. "Sorry." He focused on the sand as a warm feeling spread through him. Ryan's laugh, though brief, had come easily and sounded genuine.

"You are right, though. It's beautiful here." He pulled Kaden's hand and held it in his lap between both of his.

Kaden rolled his head to stare at Ryan. He smiled and moved closer. "Hold still." He twisted his body and, with his free hand, held Ryan's face, swept his thumb over his cheek.

Their eyes met, and Kaden found himself falling into Ryan's blue gaze. *Blue like the vast sky.* He could lose himself in them.

"There was some sand." He kept his hand on Ryan's face, gently stroked his cheek. Then he closed the gap between them.

Ryan closed his eyes, a small hitched breath falling from between his parted lips as Kaden's mouth met his.

Kaden could feel Ryan pushing back into the kiss, and for a brief moment, he forgot they were acting. Ryan was warm, responding to his kiss and touch. Acting? Was that an excuse? He'd wanted to kiss Ryan and not only for appearances.

"Ten minutes," came a call from behind them.

*Time's almost up.* Kaden breathed in as he pulled away. "I should let you prepare." He squeezed Ryan's hand, then released it. He didn't get far before Ryan caught his wrist. "Is everything okay?"

Ryan stared at his hand on Kaden.

"That was okay, right? The kiss. Carmen suggested

I…" Kaden gestured back at the house. People were on the move again.

"Of course." Ryan's grip loosened. "Carmen."

"I can stay with you for longer. If you'd like me to."

What answer he had hoped for, Kaden wasn't sure, but the moment Ryan let go of his hand, he was struck with a sense of loss.

"I'm fine."

The smile Ryan wore was unconvincing, and guilt crept into Kaden's heart. *What is this?* His emotions were getting twisted, entangled. He didn't know what else to say. "Good luck."

He made his way back to the house and up the steps to the deck. He hesitated for a moment, drew his hand over the wooden rail. Ryan hadn't moved, and suddenly he seemed so alone and lost in the broad stretch of sand.

*What am I doing?*

Kaden turned away, settled his gaze on the book he had been reading. Carmen had been right with what she'd said that morning. It was only lunchtime, and already, it was turning out to be a long day. He was exhausted.

## Chapter Eight

Ryan decided this was turning out to be the longest day in the history of long days. Starting so early, he was having makeup applied before it turned nine, and there had been delay after delay. His hair wasn't *this*, his eyes weren't *that*, and the light was apparently all over the place. Too bright, too dim, too much bounce from the sparkling ocean. The sun was too sunny, the puffy clouds causing shadows. It was one thing after another, and he was feeling the strain of too much sitting around doing nothing. Sharing company and a sandwich with Kaden had been the best part about today, and that kiss had been everything he'd needed to settle his thoughts and drag him from the torment he had been subjecting himself to.

Paul's last message to him had been a long-winded email. He should have left it where it was in the trash, but no, he'd rescued it. Why was he doing this to himself? It was a wound he couldn't stop scratching. Maybe it was a sickness.

*I forgive you.* Paul's words. He forgave Ryan for saying

those horrible things about him, for the threats to out him.

*I understand you.* They could weather the storm together. No matter what anyone else thought of Ryan, Paul would always be on his side.

*With time, if we decide we want to be together, I could speak to my father.* If it was Ryan, if he went back, one day he and Paul could step out of the shadows.

There was no mention of Luke at all. Ryan's heart hurt at that. Luke was so defensive, so wholly besotted with Paul, and Paul never even said his name once. *Don't I owe it to Luke to try and explain what is happening? Or has Paul changed?*

He'd deleted the message again, for good this time. He wanted to fill his mind with nothing but the soft warmth of Kaden's kiss. He didn't care if it was real or just an act, at that moment, it had meant everything to him, had eased his muddled heart.

Whether the kiss was enough to see him through the torture of his first interview, he didn't know, but he couldn't avoid talking to the people from a cosmetics company. They wanted to talk photoshoots and promo and skincare regimes. He already had his notes memorized, what to say about a moisturizer that he'd only used once, and hair gel that made his hair way too sticky.

Still, they were sponsors for the film, so he didn't have much choice, and while the team waited for the right kind of light, a journalist, all chirpy and in his face, decided to pounce, thrusting her phone under his nose.

"This is like everyone's dream," she began and gestured at the team of people all here for him. "You know you've made it when you have twenty people making you look good, right?"

He unpicked what she said, not sure if that was some veiled sarcasm, holding back the instant irritation.

"It takes an army," he joked. *Keep it light.*

"What can you tell us about some of the products you're using today?"

He delivered all his lines the first time, relaxing into the steady exchange of questions and answers, even going so far to crack a joke about fighting with his boyfriend over who got to use the last of the film-official shower gel.

"Can I get a photo of the two of you together for the blog post?" Sonia directed her question to one of the directors of this whole thing who was hovering, along with Kaden who stood a few feet away. He'd been watching this unfolding, standing as soon as Sonia had begun her interview, all protective boyfriend.

"Just stand together, super casual," Sonia said.

Carmen interjected then. "We're not allowing informal shots today," she warned. "Official photos only."

"One won't hurt," Kaden said and slid an arm over Ryan's shoulders. He was warm from the sun, and he leaned in, squeezing Ryan, holding him close, and smiling. Ryan melted a little, staring right into Kaden's eyes and only snapping out of it when Sonia cooed something about how cute they were. Pulling himself back to the here and now, he smiled into the camera, tilting his head until it rested on Kaden's shoulder.

"Thank you," she said, and they shook hands.

"Can I get a copy of the photo?" Kaden asked, playing his part of the doting boyfriend way too well.

"Give me your phone, and I'll forward any you took to mine." He held out a hand, and Sonia didn't even hesitate, not even watching as Kaden forwarded the photos to his phone. She left with a smile, a couple more hugs, and a thoughtful comment about how damn cute they were, and then it was just the two of them and Carmen.

Kaden pocketed his cell.

"What was all that about? That was taking things a step too far." Ryan was confused, and his words tumbled out. Why would Kaden want copies of the photos?

"Just keeping an eye on things," Kaden replied before winking and sauntering up the beach.

"At least we'll have an idea of the kind of shots she took," Carmen suggested. "Maybe that is why he did that?"

Ryan understood all of that, but he was still rattled at the heat that flooded his body when Kaden had held him. As hot as that damn kiss, Kaden touching him, Kaden's entire damn presence was messing with his head.

"Ready for the next session?" someone called over, and that was it. He was back on the clock, being told to stare moodily out over the ocean. Hell, that wasn't a hard thing to manage right now. Meeting someone he could be attracted to but wasn't allowed to, then lusting after said person anyway, was leaving him unable to regain control of his libido.

"Stupid," he muttered to himself between takes, glancing up to where Kaden was leaning on the porch, staring down at him. The weight of that stare made his face grow hot, so he forced himself to ignore Kaden and concentrated on getting this day over and done with.

"Okay, we're done with the photos," someone announced.

Ryan didn't care who it was; he was taking the announcement at face value, and made all the right noises, thanking people for their time today. Then he stalked up to the house, slumping into the first chair he came to.

"Here you go." Kaden handed him a tall glass of icy soda and dropped a kiss on his head as he did. He took the seat next to him. They sat in silence, watching the teams dismantle equipment with the beach returning to normal. The tide was washing away the messed-up sand at the shoreline, and the rock they'd made him sit on when he had to do the moody thing was being splashed with seawater.

"That went okay," Kaden said. "Or at least it looked okay from where I was sitting."

"Well, there weren't any leading questions about the fact that I threatened to out someone, so yeah, I call that a win." He yawned and slid lower in the chair. Carmen joined them, talking to Kaden as Ryan closed his eyes and focused on the breeze from the sea, the sound of birds, and the warmth from the early evening sun.

"Ryan, I need you to post the photo," she said, and Ryan blinked the sleep away, yawning again and moving to sit upright.

"What?"

"This, you need to post it." She handed Ryan his phone, and he fumbled to hold it before focusing on the screen, which unlocked as he checked.

"What photo?" He was used to doing what Carmen asked him, and this photo must've been relevant if she wanted it done now.

She took the phone from him, and after a few taps, she handed it back. His Instagram app was open, with a photo of him and Kaden looking at each other adoringly.

"Is this the one the woman who interviewed us took?" He peered at it, seeing the way he was connecting with Kaden and the protective way Kaden held him. It was like a perfect still, and posting this sent a message that he and Kaden were a thing. He hesitated over what to write, then typed in a general message *photoshoot on the beach, living the life with the bf*. Was that flowery enough, did it sound as if he was in love? Did it make him a good person now to have a fake photo of him and Kaden out there for the world to see? He added a heart and a smiley face, then considered the hashtags he should add. They were on a beach; they were together; they needed to emphasize the gay couple headline.

"Is this okay?" He passed the phone to Carmen.

She read the contents out loud. "Photoshoot on the beach, living the life with the bf, heart, smiley face, hashtag beachlove hashtag loveislove hashtag pride." She typed something else and passed the phone back. "I added a reference to the film. You can send that. Right, I have a meeting. You two crazy kids going to be okay?"

"We'll be good," Kaden said as Ryan pressed post, holding the phone up when there was no instant connection, and watched as it posted to his legion of fans, many of them from his soap opera days. Then he turned the phone off and laid it on the table. It used to be, when he'd first had social media, that he would watch the numbers climb, judging what he posted by the number of likes, judging his success or failures on how many comments he got. Now he hardly ever used it, not after the messages he'd had from people who wanted to comment on his recent fuckup.

He waited to feel sleepy again, maybe grab a nap, but he was restless, and thinking about the people out there who hated him put him on edge.

"I'm going for a walk," he announced, not surprised when Kaden stood as well.

"Okay if I join you?"

"Yeah." He could do with the company.

Kaden extended his hand. "We should hold hands in case there are cameras."

They linked hands, which felt odd. Kaden was right —they were on an empty stretch of land, but they did have neighbors, albeit some way along the beach.

They headed for the shoreline, in among the rocks, paddling in the water and finally both sitting on the huge rock where he'd posed earlier.

"We should do a dusk photo later, on the steps of the house or something," Kaden said.

"You're always so focused," Ryan observed and stared down at their linked hands. It wasn't as if there was any way people could see their joined hands now, with their backs to everything and sitting so close, but Kaden hadn't let go, and Ryan liked the touch.

"It's my job," Kaden said and bumped shoulders with him before shuffling a little to face Ryan.

"About the kissing…" Ryan began and then stopped. Talking about their kisses and what he felt about them was not a sensible thing to do.

"What about the kissing?" Kaden was so damn serious. "Do we need to do more?"

Ryan cleared his throat. "No. Yes. I don't know."

Kaden tightened his grip. "What's wrong?"

"It's just that… look, what if I told you that I *liked* kissing you?"

"Sorry?"

Great. Shock and horror was the worst kind of response.

Ryan shook off Kaden's hold and clambered down off the rock, splashing to the shore and heading up the beach.

"Wait up," Kaden called, but Ryan was scarlet with embarrassment and already working out a way to hide in his room forever.

Kaden jogged past him and blocked his way. "Ryan, talk to me."

"It's nothing," he lied and attempted to sidestep Kaden, tripping over his own feet and Kaden's and ending up on his ass on the sand. Kaden followed him down, pulled him into a hug, and kissed him. Not for pretend, not because anyone was watching them, but just for the taste of the kiss. They kissed for the longest time, lost in the moment, and when Kaden cradled his face and held him still to deepen the kiss, it was the most intensely erotic moment of Ryan's adult life.

He smiled at Ryan, kissed the tip of his nose.

"What if I was to tell you that I liked kissing you too?"

They walked up the beach, holding hands, but this time it was more natural. It was the kind of thing two men who had kissed each other on the beach would do.

"What's on the itinerary for tomorrow," Kaden asked when they reached the house.

"The first day of the promotional interviews and then drinks in the evening. Are you ready for that? It might be another long day of sitting around for you again."

"I can't wait," Kaden said.

They took the dusk photo Kaden had suggested, then kissed again, a few feet inside the door, but it didn't go any further. Kaden found a movie for them to watch, but Ryan was too tired and fell asleep on the sofa. When he woke, it was light outside, and he'd slept through the entire night covered in a blanket. There was a note propped up in front of him.

*Didn't want to wake you. I hope that was okay. Gone for a run.*

"Why are you sleeping out here?" Carmen asked from the kitchen.

"Fell asleep watching a movie."

No point in telling her anything yet, even if the memory of the kisses did make him smile.

## Chapter Nine

"It's how I imagine speed dating goes." Kaden rested his elbows on the breakfast bar and swiveled his hips to turn the seat of the tall stool.

"Imagine? So you've never tried it?" Carmen said in a low voice as she kept watch over Ryan from a distance as he gave his final interview.

It had been a day of interview after interview, a string of people from the media asking the same questions over and over.

*How does he manage to look so interested all the time?*

Ryan's enthusiasm had never waned. At least not outwardly. He'd laughed, exchanged pleasantries with ease, and came across as upbeat, positive, and excited for the movie's release.

Kaden leaned his head and looked up at Carmen. "And you have?"

Carmen pouted. "Maybe once or twice. We can't all be lucky enough to find love in a place we would normally frequent." Her pout became a frown as she eyed her brother. "Then again, sometimes it turns out to be not so lucky."

Inhaling slowly, Kaden settled his gaze on Ryan. He was sure there was a tale behind him and Paul, how they'd met, how they'd become a *thing*, but it wasn't one he cared to hear, nor did he think Ryan would want to tell it. He couldn't deny, however, being curious as to why their relationship had taken the direction it had. What was it that went through a person's head that they could treat another cruelly?

"Right." Carmen's expression changed to something more determined. "Time to call time."

"This is the last one?" Kaden sat up and stretched his neck from side to side.

"For today."

"Right." His shoulders slumped.

"Something wrong?" Carmen ducked her head, leaned in closer. There was a concern in her gaze, fear for him, and it surprised him.

Kaden shook his head. "Just feeling a bit guilty."

"Guilty?" She raised an eyebrow, and her aura shifted to that of Ryan's protector. "What did you do?"

"Huh? Nothing." He waved his hand in front of him. "I was thinking about how you're paying for me to sit around this place. I feel as though I should be doing something more."

Carmen picked up her cell phone, and for a moment, stared at the blank screen. "I think we both know it's more than just that." She glanced over to the staging area for the interviews.

Behind Ryan was the poster for the movie, both him and it framed by the view of the beach from the window.

"You paint a picture," she said. "You're a loving partner who stands at Ryan's side despite the recent upset. And that is something. Or at least the something he needs right now." With that, she headed over to Ryan, ready to call time on the day.

Kaden raised his fingers to his mouth and touched his parted lips gently. He thought about last night, about the kiss that had been nothing to do with painting a picture. He'd tried to get things clear in his head, to figure out what he wanted and needed to say to Ryan given their current working situation. He'd taken a long run, looked out on the vast, open stretch of water, and yet nothing had settled in his mind, and when he had gotten back to the beach house, they were no longer alone.

There was nothing he could do for now. There wasn't enough time for any meaningful conversation before they were onto the next thing. Tonight they were attending another party, though supposedly more intimate and hosted by the movie's director. Maybe after a glass of champagne, he and Ryan could talk more easily about the moment they had shared and where things stood for them, going forward.

"So... where are we going?" Kaden asked after ten minutes in the car. He slouched and spread his legs. "Some fancy house in Santa Monica, right?"

Ryan nodded. "Fancier than the beach house, I'm sure."

Kaden glanced out the window. "How are you feeling? Did you manage to rest, or had a chance to take a nap or something in between?"

"What am I? A toddler?" Ryan said, and laughed. "I'm fine. It wasn't too bad today. I don't mind when all the questions stay work-focused." He rested his hand in the space between them. "With what happened, there's always a chance of an unwelcome commentary."

Kaden lowered his gaze, looked at Ryan's hand. He wanted to reach out, lace his fingers through Ryan's, offer comfort.

*Why don't I?*

There was nothing to stop him. He could, right? It was okay to reach for something, someone he might want to call his own, wasn't it? *Might.* Ryan wasn't in a position to take a chance on might. Kaden was sure Ryan needed something more to be able to open his heart to someone again.

When it came down to it, Kaden wasn't good at letting people in. Trust was fragile, like a thin layer of ice over water, and he didn't want to endure the heart-rending chill of the freezing waters below, not again.

He glanced back out the window as they fell silent. He couldn't stay like this forever. On the outside, he acted confident, had handled the kiss with charming ease. Inside, however, the betrayed boy still lingered, tarnishing his view of other people and their intentions toward him.

*Those damned parents of mine.*

Kaden closed his eyes and filled his lungs. *Screw it.* Facing the front of the car, he lowered his hand to the seat, then reached out until his hand bumped Ryan's. He waited, giving Ryan time to react. If Ryan had wanted to, he could have pulled away, but he didn't. *This is okay, right?* Kaden clasped Ryan's hand. He kept his eyes on the reflection of the lights they passed, in the center partition.

"Can we talk later?" Ryan said.

Kaden looked his way and was surprised to find Ryan leaning toward him. "If that's what you want." He studied the changing shadows on Ryan's face and swore the man's bottom lip trembled.

He hesitated, doubts crept into his head. Was he a complication Ryan didn't need?

In the end, it was Ryan who made the next move. Reaching across, he cupped Kaden's cheek. Their eyes met as he swiped his thumb across Kaden's lips. "There was some sand," he repeated Kaden's line from the previous day.

Kaden couldn't help but smile. "Sand, huh? Gets everywhere." He leaned as far as his seat belt would allow, meeting Ryan halfway. They kissed for a long moment, and with words eluding him, all Kaden could think was how *good* it felt.

Ryan leaned back. "So, later?"

Kaden nodded. "Okay. Let's talk."

A few hours had passed since arriving at the luxurious Santa Monica property. Kaden had slipped away from the crowded room and was sitting on a bench out on the patio. The energy of the party was mellowing. Kaden rotated the tumbler in his hand, covering the ice in a wave of bourbon. Alcohol had taken its toll on some of the guests. With a sigh, he turned away from the darkness that had once held a beautiful view of the ocean, and settled instead for gazing up at the large house behind him. Large. That was pretty much the only thought he had about the building. That and the fact that he was envious of its space, its brightness, and how it looked out on the water from its nestled position on a slope.

"Give it back, Manny." A woman giggled from across the patio. A man was standing beside her, holding her purse out over the pool.

"For a kiss?" The man hooked the strap on his finger and swung it around.

The woman pouted, and the man receded.

"Okay. Okay. I'm sorry. Don't be mad. Here."

Kaden raised an eyebrow as the woman snatched the bag, then grabbed the man by his tie. She yanked hard, moving the man toward the house. "You can kiss me when we get home."

*What was that about?* Kaden stared into his glass. *Ugh. I wanna leave too.*

"Hey." Ryan sounded cheerful as he sidestepped in front of Kaden. "Thought I'd lost you."

"You seemed to be having fun socializing, so I decided to get some air." He wondered if Ryan's ability to relax and mingle had to do with the people at the party or rather the one person who wasn't on the guest list? Seeing Paul had caused quite the upset, but from all outward appearances, Ryan looked to be coping.

Ryan sat beside him. He smiled, then took Kaden's drink from him, had a sip. "Oh. How do you drink that?" He held it out to Kaden and grimaced. "I'm about ready to get out of here." As he spoke, he moved closer to rest his hand on Kaden's leg. "You?"

Ryan's hand left a heated trail through Kaden's pants as he slid it across to his inner thigh. There was color in Ryan's cheeks and alcohol on his breath as he leaned in, circling Kaden's neck to pull him forward and initiating a kiss. Kaden closed his eyes, parted his lips and accepted the sloppy intimacy.

"Are you drunk?" Kaden asked when the kiss ended. Ryan's face was still close to his.

Ryan shook his head, then pressed an openmouthed kiss to Kaden jaw, his teeth grazing Kaden's skin. "I guess some of it is an act, but"—he sat back, ducked his head with a comfortable smile—"I guess I found it easier tonight, like it was okay to be normal." He moved his hand upward, his pinky finger extending and brushing against the tightening material across Kaden's crotch.

*This is dangerous.* Kaden rested his hand over Ryan's and gripped it. "You shouldn't."

Ryan relaxed his hand before trying to pull back. "Sorry. I didn't… I thought…" He turned away.

Kaden placed his drink on the ground, reaffirmed his hold on Ryan, and tugged his arm, pulling him into an embrace. Ryan stiffened in surprise. "Let's try that again," he said at Ryan's ear as he hugged him. "You shouldn't do that here."

"What?"

"I know why I'm here, the image you want to present. But this…" He turned as he checked who was nearby. He pressed Ryan's hand against the growing bulge in the front of his pants. "This isn't it. You should think of yourself more." He cast his gaze sideways and to the crowd inside. One ill-timed snap from a cell phone, one post on social media and something intimate, private from Ryan's life would once again be out there for anyone to see, to comment on. "These feelings, whatever they are and how we choose to act on them, should stay private. Between just us."

Ryan acknowledged the people around them, then returned his focus to Kaden. He moved his fingers, the motion teasing against Kaden's strained pants.

Kaden released him and picked up his drink. He downed the diluted whiskey. Getting to his feet, he held out his hand. "You wanted to get out of here, right?"

A smile spread across Ryan's face as he took Kaden by the hand. "I do."

It wasn't long before they were in a car heading for the beach house. Ryan sat in the middle of the back seat with his head resting against Kaden's shoulder.

*Is he already asleep?*

Kaden pushed Ryan's bangs back from his face to check. Ryan's eyes were shut, his features reflecting the relaxed atmosphere that filled the car.

*What am I doing?*

He withdrew his hand carefully, not wanting to disturb him. He stared out the window and thought back to the patio and the memory of Ryan's touch on his leg.

*So warm.*

The sensation lingered, and he realized it wasn't just the memory.

*I guess he's not asleep.*

Kaden slouched a little, leaned his elbow on the door, and pushed his fist to his mouth. Ryan had his fingers on his crotch, was gripping the line of his erection through the material. A soft grunt escaped his lips, and he eyed the partition. The thought of someone being on the other side scared but also excited him.

Ryan didn't lift his head, made no significant

movements. He remained pressed to Kaden's side as he traced the line of Kaden's dick, squeezing balls and shaft. A few moments more and he was seeking access, working the button open on Kaden's pants, and slipping beneath the waistband of his underwear.

"Guh." Kaden made another low sound. His lack of control frustrated him. Kaden shifted as Ryan gave his erection space to spring upward. He bit the knuckle of his index finger as Ryan wrapped his hand around his length.

*Seriously?* His body tensed, reacted far more quickly than he'd expected. He bit down as he imagined each steady stroke on his cock, imagined what it would be like to strip the guy bare, have him vulnerable, open beneath him. Desire throbbed through him, his thoughts muddling, and he couldn't stave off the emotional rush that heated his blood. He tried hard—thought of anything and everything that wasn't Ryan's hand on him, and then just as quickly as he'd begun, Ryan stopped.

He moved away, adjusting himself in his pants, and thumped his head on the headrest, groaning quietly.

"Not here," he muttered, more to himself than Kaden. "Sorry," he whispered. Kaden glanced down at him. He looked anything but sorry, the streetlights they passed illuminating the curve of his lips. "I mean—"

Kaden pressed a finger to Ryan's lips, then trailed that finger down his chin, his throat, then circled his left nipple, brushing firmly, then leaving his hand there.

"You're not sorry at all," Kaden murmured and then pinched his nipple, gratified when Ryan groaned and squirmed.

Turnabout was fair play.

## Chapter Ten

Somehow they made it back to the beach house without coming in their pants. God knows how because all Ryan could think about was getting his hands on Kaden, preferably with fewer clothes in the way.

*Maybe we should talk about this?* His treacherous brain threatened to wreck everything. If they began to talk, then Ryan would get all flustered, mess it up, his brain wouldn't work, and words would just fall out randomly. That was part of the reason Paul had had such an influence on him. Paul had realized that under the sexy TV actor with a future was a bumbling idiot kid who wasn't even that good at sex.

*Who even pushes their hand down their pretend boyfriend's pants?*

Another pinch of his nipple and Ryan slid farther down in the seat, widening his legs, anything to give his cock room, but he didn't touch himself or Kaden. He wanted to, but he knew he'd fuck it up, as much as he knew night followed day.

Paul's voice poked into his thoughts. *"For fuck's sake, Ryan, what are you? A virgin or something?"*

*I will not let him in my head. I will not let him in my head.*

They reached the beach house, and Kaden was thanking the driver and opening the door all at the same time. He burst out of the car, then reached in and grabbed Ryan's hand, tugging him out and leading him to the front door. He had the key in the lock in an instant and then pulled Ryan inside, pressing him against the nearest wall and holding him there as he locked the door with his other hand.

Then it was game over.

All the insecurities, the worries, and Paul's words fled.

Kaden lifted him a little until he was on tiptoes, encouraged Ryan to wrap his arms around his neck, then pushed his thigh between Ryan's legs, all the while kissing him deeply. The kisses were everything; they didn't stop. This wasn't just sex in a hallway. Ryan felt as if Kaden was claiming him, making his mark, holding him still so he couldn't even squirm away.

But what he could do was grind against Kaden's thick thigh, and coupled with the kisses and the fact that he couldn't move, Ryan was in heaven.

*See, Paul, I* can *do this.*

But *his* voice was there as well, belittling all Ryan's efforts. *Yeah, and look at Kaden doing all the work.*

He forced that away, lost himself in kissing, not even aware when Kaden released his hold and led him from the hallway down to his bedroom. Once inside, Kaden headed for the bed, began removing his clothes, until gloriously nude, he turned back to Ryan.

Ryan, who hadn't moved from the door, who stood

there like an idiot, his erection tenting his dress pants, and his inability to get past the thoughts in his head, terrifyingly real.

Kaden padded toward him, concern on his face. "Are you okay?" he asked, and Ryan wasn't sure if he'd expected an answer, but he was getting one anyway.

"No, I'm... I can't do this."

Maybe he didn't sound anxious to end this, or perhaps what his body wanted was giving off vibes, but Kaden didn't stop his advance and captured his face in his hands.

"Then we won't," he murmured. "It's okay, Ryan."

Desperation curled inside Ryan, a clawing need to get onto that bed with Kaden and have honest sex, but the fear was there.

Kaden kissed him and ran his thumbs across Ryan's cheekbones. "It's all okay," he reassured. "I'll make us a drink."

Then he left, eased Ryan from the door, and left. He hadn't sounded angry or resentful. He'd accepted from Ryan's statement that sex wasn't happening right now, and it was okay with him if Ryan didn't want to.

*I* do *want to.*

Ryan stalked to the patio doors to the balcony and threw them open, staring outside at the ocean beyond. The moon was fat and bright, and the night sky was speckled with stars. This place was beautiful. Add the sound of waves, and Ryan had every ingredient to find some peace so he could think.

Paul had never stopped. On the occasions when Ryan had been exhausted or low or needed some alone time, he would push for what he wanted. Most of the time, it had been sex; other times it had been parading

Ryan around a succession of parties where drinking was the norm and recreational drugs the dessert of choice.

*In Paul's defense, he never made you take drugs.*

Anger washed over Ryan. Why was he excusing any of his time with Paul? Why did his mind tell him that Paul was a good man for not expecting him to join in with the drugs? What about the times that sex had hurt? Or the hundred other tiny things that Paul had done to him? The comments on his clothes or his hair, humiliations in front of his peers, the choices he'd made on Ryan's behalf.

None of it was good.

Bit by bit, Paul had stripped Ryan's confidence, told him he was too vanilla, too young, too *everything*.

"You're an idiot, Ryan," he concluded in the safety of the dark. His cell vibrated, and he pulled it out immediately when he saw it was Carmen. His sister's timing was perfect as if she'd sensed he needed someone to talk to.

"Hey, Ry, how did the party go?"

All his energy fled then, and he sat on the raised wooden deck, his back to the upright. "It's not good."

"The party? I thought it was a cast thing? Shit, was Paul there? Wait, is this even a Paul thing, or is this a paparazzi thing? Do I need to get the—?"

"I was going to have sex," Ryan blurted out, then hid behind his hands because fuck, he was outside his room and anyone who happened to be passing might hear him. Not that people could easily pass. It would likely only be Kaden, and that was even worse.

"Okay," Carmen sounded cautious. "With...?"

"Kaden. Who else would it be?" Ryan whispered.

"Great," was her enthusiastic first response. "Wait, what do you mean you *were* going to have sex?"

"Paul got inside my head, and I fucking lost it like an idiot."

Ryan heard some rustling as Carmen moved around her room and then the soft exhalation of breath as she sat down. She was used to his meltdowns and always made herself comfortable and ready to listen. He'd lost count of the number of times she'd listened to him list the things he couldn't make sense of. She'd always been the level-headed one, and he'd come to rely on her excellent counsel.

But then it hit him. Why was he thinking of talking this through with his sister? This was raw, passionate need, and he shouldn't be debating it, particularly with his sister. Why was he sitting in the dark, ready to unburden the same insecurities she'd heard a hundred times before? Kaden was somewhere in the house, and they could be having sex right now.

Why let Paul's shit cause him to miss out on a night with Kaden?

"What am I doing?" he said instead.

"I don't—"

"I'll talk to you tomorrow, sis. I'm going to find Kaden."

"You are?" She sounded surprised. Then her tone changed. "Go get 'im, Ry."

"Love you."

"Love you too."

Determined, he dropped his cell onto the bedside table, then went looking for Kaden, finding him in the kitchen, dressed in shorts and a T-shirt, standing at the counter, two hot chocolates in front of him. Kaden smiled at him.

"I was just coming to bring these in but thought you might need a bit more time—"

Ryan held out a hand. "I'm not good at this, I know that, but…" He stopped and waited as Kaden took his hand.

"It's okay, Ryan. We don't have to—"

Ryan climbed him like a tree. He shook off their laced fingers, wrapping his hands behind Kaden's neck and pushing him to the kitchen wall. He was hard, Kaden was hard, and they kissed until they ran out of air. It was him who took the initiative, moving backward into the table, then a chair, then a doorway, stumbling and kissing until they were in his room, with the doors wide open to the ocean, the summer air warming the room. They stripped each other hurriedly; clothes left where they fell. Then they tumbled onto the mattress in the moonlit place. They kissed and rutted, and Kaden had Ryan flat on his back, Ryan gripping Kaden's ass and his legs spread wide. He wanted Kaden right *now*.

"I need you to fuck me," he said and waited for Kaden to turn down the offer. But Kaden wasn't at all hesitant, and his response was immediate.

"Condoms? Lube?"

"In my toiletry bag in the bathroom—"

Kaden didn't even wait for the end of the explanation, and in no time at all, he was back at the bed with the condoms and lube, both of which he tossed to the bed before settling back between Ryan's spread legs.

But they didn't go straight to the fucking. Instead,

Kaden spent the longest time kissing, from lips to throat and back again.

"I can't get enough of the taste of you," Kaden murmured, deepening the kiss. Ryan wriggled and pushed because he wanted more than just kisses, and *finally*, Kaden got the message, and he moved his attention lower to worry at Ryan's nipples, then pressing his lips to Ryan's belly and taking the tip of Ryan's cock into his mouth. With slick-lubed fingers, he pressed inside Ryan, sucking him, and Ryan was lost. He didn't know whether to push down on Kaden's fingers or thrust up into the tight heat of Kaden's mouth. He settled for holding as still as he could and groaning with need. He was so close to coming, had been on edge since they started, and he wanted Kaden inside him when that happened. None of this felt like any kind of sex he'd had before. Kaden was prepping him, stretching him, kissing, stroking, surrounding Ryan and not stopping.

When he thought he was done, when he was so close he warned Kaden, the tempo changed. Kaden stopped touching him, moved back and away, wiped his hands, and rolled on a condom.

"You're so sexy lying there," he murmured as he looked at Ryan. "I could stare at you all night."

Ryan didn't want to talk; he wanted action, and he pressed his hands on his inner thighs and rolled up and back.

"Please," he demanded, his voice scratchy.

He winced at the first touch, recalling other times when the discomfort had outweighed pleasure, and Kaden stopped, moved gently, kissed him, rocking until Ryan relaxed, and then pushed a little. More kisses, and then more burn, until he was in, and Ryan's tight chest loosened.

"Ryan?" Kaden asked, staring at him.

"Please... move," Ryan said, and Kaden shuffled forward, in hard and then retreating as Ryan gripped his knees. Over and over, Kaden moved, and Ryan wanted more kisses, but right now, the sensation of Kaden inside him stole his ability to ask.

"Fuck," Kaden said, resting on his hands and leaning as far as he could to kiss Ryan, like that, exchanging sloppy, heated kisses. The sounds of sex filled the room, and with his cock trapped between them, he was coming.

Kaden followed quickly, still kissing Ryan through his own orgasm, and then they were apart, Kaden falling to the mattress, removing the condom, and wiping at the cooling mess on his and Ryan's belly. Then he gathered Ryan in his arms.

"Wow," he said into Ryan's hair, "just, wow."

"Uh-huh," Ryan replied because it seemed as if he'd lost the power of speech.

"We need to do that again."

"Uh-huh. Sleep first."

Wrapped in Kaden's arms, he closed his eyes, lulled into sleep by good sex and the sound of the ocean. Tomorrow he'd worry if he'd been good enough, deal with any fallout, but tonight he was stealing this sensation of being needed and keeping it for himself.

## Chapter Eleven

*What's that sound?*

Kaden squeezed his eyes shut. He didn't want to wake yet. Instead, he wanted to stay in the comfortable dream that was Ryan and last night. His memory was filled with everything Ryan from his touch to his scent, every sight, and every sound.

Gradually, Kaden stirred and opened his eyes. The sound he could hear was that of his phone. He checked the bedside but found nothing.

*Where did I leave it?*

He leaned up on his elbow, tracking the sound to his pile of crumpled clothing on the floor. "Hah," he said with a sigh and hung over the side of the bed, trying and failing to hook the leg of his shorts. The bed was warm, and he didn't want to leave it, but he was going to have to. With a groan, he rolled out of bed, scooped up his clothes, and freed his phone from his shorts' pocket.

"Hello?" he answered. His voice was uneven, hoarse, and he cleared his throat.

"Good morning." The voice was bright, loud, familiar.

Kaden scratched his head, briefly lowering the phone to check the caller ID. "Rowan?"

"You were expecting someone else?" Rowan sounded far too awake.

"I didn't look before I answered." Kaden stared at the painting on the wall. An abstract piece made up of blue semi-circles.

*Is it supposed to mean something?*

"Are you still half-asleep?" Rowan said.

"What do you want?"

"Well, aren't you grumpy."

Kaden sighed. "It's barely after six."

"Six? Oh. You're not in New York right now, are you?"

Kaden rubbed at his eyes. "No, I'm not." There was a restless sound behind him. He checked over his shoulder. Ryan had rolled over.

*So that really did happen.* Last night had been more than just some wistful dream. He pushed at his brow, tried to ignore the hollow feeling in his chest. *What is this?*

"Kaden?"

"What? Sorry." He'd gotten distracted. "It's fine," he said, making sure to lower his voice. "What do you need?" He eased himself from the room and pulled the door shut behind him, then went to the bathroom.

"I'm just checking in. Making sure everything is okay on your end, the usual."

"So you're after some gossip?" Kaden concluded.

Rowan made an incredulous sound. "I would never."

He laughed. "But if you happened upon some, I'm all for hearing it."

Kaden sat on the side of the bath. He shuddered and brushed his hand over his naked thighs, appreciating the warmth of his palm. "I see. Well, I've nothing to report in particular. Hit a couple of bumps, but we seem to be back on track."

"Bumps?" Rowan's tone turned serious, more business-like, as he switched to the first-class PA Gideon relied on him to be. "Anything we should know about and need to manage?"

"I don't believe so. We stumbled upon Ryan's ex, the one I've been told the video is about. I might have lacked a little subtlety when handling him, but I think we're good now." He smiled to himself. "Probably more than good." There was a break in the conversation. "Rowan?"

"Sorry. You surprised me for a moment."

"I did?" Kaden stilled his hand. What had he said?

"It almost sounded like you'd taken an interest in Mr. Levesque." Rowan snorted. "But that can't be right."

"An interest in…?" It was true Kaden rarely took the bait when Rowan tried to lure him into pointless small talk. He didn't care for it and didn't want Rowan seeing it as an invitation to poke around in his private affairs. Kaden side-eyed the closed door, thought about Ryan lying in the other room. "It's the job. Same as always."

"Yes, yes. Don't get involved. Don't get attached. Don't step beyond what's laid out in the contract."

Kaden sighed. "Are you saying I shouldn't follow the rules?"

"And whose rules would they be?"

*Ah, that tone. I'm getting drawn in.*

Gideon's rules for all his employees, family or not, were simple. It boiled down to *don't piss off the client*. And in the same way, clients were instructed to *don't piss off the staff*. The simplest way to do that was to follow the contract. No complications, no entanglements, just the job that needed doing. Kaden found it more comfortable that way.

He worried his lower lip and pressed his clenched fist to his chest. *Then why didn't you follow the rules this time?* Something was different. His feelings about Ryan were different from any he'd had in a long time.

Kaden wasn't in the mood to be led any further into an awkward conversation with Rowan, and yet he wondered if he should disclose what had happened last night. What went on behind closed doors while on the job stayed there, but this was a celebrity he was dealing with.

*Ryan is a celebrity.* Why was that fact making itself so startlingly obvious to him? So what exactly was last night? His chest hurt. Sex could *only* be sex, but when he looked at Ryan, he wanted to envelop him in his arms, make him his. *What is wrong with me?* He scratched at his head, then raised his face to stare at the light fixture.

"Are you okay?" Rowan asked.

"Yes." Kaden knew he'd answered too fast after the long pause. "If there's nothing else, I wouldn't mind trying to grab an extra hour of sleep. They start things pretty early around here." Rowan was silent. "So, is that everything?"

"Can I say one thing, and then I'll let you go?"

"I get the feeling you will anyway."

Rowan sighed. "I know you don't enjoy talking

about yourself, and I annoy the hell out of you, but if something is bothering you… I don't mind listening. Or, you know, talk to Gideon or somebody."

Kaden pushed his thighs together and leaned forward. He'd already figured Rowan would be aware Gideon knew at least the summary version of his circumstances, his history. But that was the past. It didn't define him, or that's what he kept telling himself. His father had walked away, and his mom had taken things out on him. It had hurt. It made him question the strength of his connections with people. If his own family could hurt him, then anyone could. "That it?"

"Yes, that's it. We'll see you when you get back."

"Okay." He closed his eyes. "And Rowan? Thanks."

"You're welcome." Rowan ended the call.

Kaden lowered his cell phone and placed it on the bath edge. He rested his hand over his chin, gently stroked his thumb back and forth along the line of his jaw. His thoughts went to last night and Ryan. Sex had been amazing. Ryan, his body so responsive to every one of Kaden's touches. He should've been happy. He should've been basking in the afterglow.

*And yet instead there's this ache.* As if a cavity had opened in his chest.

With each day he spent with Ryan, Kaden had seen more and more he liked about him, and he believed there was enough between them that he'd wanted to let Ryan in. Let him see beneath the surface. The sex, the moment they'd shared, had been filled with emotions from both sides. Kaden was sure of that.

*And yet…* What if the sex was a step to something more between them? What if down the line, Ryan ended up being another person who ended up disappointing him?

"Fuck it." Kaden roughly rubbed both his hands over his head. He was getting ahead of himself. Not everyone in his life turned out to be an asshole. "What the hell do I think about this crap for?" He opened his eyes. "There's a hot guy in the room next door. A hot guy you like and who gives the impression he likes you too. This is why you've been alone for so long. You think everyone is going to fuck you over. Do you know how crazy that sounds?" He sighed. "Probably as crazy as talking to yourself in the bathroom."

Standing, he caught sight of his reflection in the mirror. "Crazy." He picked up his phone. With any luck, Ryan was still sleeping so Kaden could curl up and hold him for a while longer.

He pulled open the door and stopped.

*Kill me now.*

"Good—" Carmen's gaze went south. "Morning." She pouted and averted her gaze toward the ceiling. "Erm…" She backed up and grabbed one of the cushions off the sofa. "Here."

Kaden caught the cushion and used it to cover his crotch. "Hi. This isn't… I mean…" He blew out a long breath.

"Is it safe?" Carmen squinted as she lowered her eyes warily.

"I didn't hear you come in." Kaden eyed the door to Ryan's room.

She pushed her glasses up her nose. "I was being quiet as we'd agreed on half-past."

Kaden checked his phone. It was seventeen past. "Right. More movie interviews."

Carmen nodded. "It's the last day today. I'm sure you remember these are being held at a hotel."

"I remember."

"We'll be meeting up with Imelda beforehand." She rested her hand on her hip, raised her eyebrow as she stared toward the open door of the bedroom Kaden had been assigned. "Were you on the sofa again?"

"Well…" He didn't know what to say.

She cocked her head and side-eyed Ryan's door. A smile teased the corners of her lips. "You've got twenty minutes." She collected her purse from the kitchen counter. "I'll be out on the deck."

Kaden side-stepped to Ryan's door, tossing the cushion back onto the sofa, then entered the bedroom. He halted when he met Ryan's eyes.

"Hey," Ryan said and leaned up on his elbow.

"Hey." Kaden sat on the side of the bed. "Did you sleep okay?"

Ryan nodded as he rubbed his eyes beneath his messy bangs.

*Cute.*

Kaden lay down and lifted his arm for Ryan to nestle against him. "So that you know, Carmen's here."

"She is. Oh, God." Ryan hid his face against Kaden.

"You okay?" Kaden rested his hand on Ryan's head.

"I'm so embarrassed," he mumbled into Kaden's chest.

"You're embarrassed? She saw me naked."

Ryan chuckled and rested his arm over Kaden's waist. "Fine, you win." Breathing in, he lifted his head. "Too hot." He rolled away and onto his back. "I guess if Carmen's here, that means I need to get out of bed."

"She did say we had twenty minutes." Kaden moved

closer to Ryan. He ran his hand idly down Ryan's chest, stomach, and beneath the covers, stopping at the line of Ryan's pubic hair. He stroked the smooth skin of Ryan's hips, smiling as he elicited a laugh and Ryan squirmed beneath his touch.

"Was last night, okay?" He leaned over Ryan, pressed a series of kisses to his forehead, his nose, his lips.

Ryan nodded, reached up to cup Kaden's jaw. His features were relaxed, his gaze warming. "It was good for you too, right?"

The focus in Ryan's expression was not of someone who was already done with Kaden and left him believing that even if their relationship turned out to be a short-lived affair of sex and comfort, Ryan wouldn't push him aside. Instead, Ryan seemed unsure of himself and more concerned as to whether Kaden was satisfied.

*I was overthinking it.*

Kaden gripped Ryan's wrist and, in a single swift motion, was sitting over him. He slid his hand upward to lace their fingers together. Taking Ryan's other hand as well, Kaden applied a little pressure and held them both down against the pillow. "I have no complaints." He kissed Ryan, who arched his back and canted his hips underneath him. With a sigh, Kaden lifted his head, met Ryan's needy gaze. "So, twenty minutes?" Another kiss. "Wanna make out some more?"

Ryan seemed conflicted. "What about Carmen—?"

Kaden shut Ryan up with a kiss. "Guess we just need to be quiet." He smiled but noted Ryan's hesitance, the way he shifted his focus to the closed door and twisted his hands as if wanting to be free.

"It's okay," he reassured and released Ryan's hands

to sit back. "Only if you want to because I'm game for cuddles if you'd prefer."

"Really?" Ryan's body relaxed. "It's okay?"

"Of course."

"If you're sure, then…" Ryan wrapped his arms around Kaden's waist as he sat up. "Cuddles sound nice."

Kaden stroked Ryan's hair gently. Ryan was warm, and he rested his head against Kaden's chest. "Sounds good to me too."

## Chapter Twelve

This was the last day, the final interview, and Ryan shared the room with Imelda, who held court and took all the difficult questions from him.

Until that was, the interviewer went down *that* road.

It had started innocently enough, with Kaden standing just behind the camera, giving silent support, and the interviewer asking a question that Ryan had been expecting.

"What is it like working with Imelda?"

Given this was the third film in the franchise, and he'd worked with her closely on all of them, this was a question he could answer in his sleep.

"Easy," he said and smiled. "She makes it easy for all of us to make the best film possible."

Imelda patted his arm and leaned in to press a kiss to his cheek. "Thank you, sweetheart," she said, which was another of the standard replies. Not that Ryan had been lying. She did make things easy and liked it when the younger and newer actors acknowledged her help.

The interviewer nodded, checked down with her

notes, long wavy hair falling around her face, and then with that same smile, she stared at Ryan.

"In this installment, do we find a resolution to the cliffhanger at the end of the last film?"

Ryan kept it light. "Spoiler alert," he teased. "You know I can't tell you that."

"What about your character's big secret?" The interviewer leaned forward, tucking her hair behind an ear. At this point, Ryan suspected nothing was wrong and was relaxed and enjoying the banter.

He moved as if he was going to explain something, but at the last moment, he sat back.

"That will have to stay a secret until you see the film," he said.

She pouted, in that cute way that made him relax, and then the pout disappeared, and abruptly, she was focused.

"What about your personal life, Ryan? What about the video threatening to expose a real-life secret?"

Silence.

Ryan couldn't process the situation fast enough. Imelda stood, Kaden moved in front of the camera, and security formed a wall, and Ryan didn't know what to say.

"Who was the video about, Ryan?" she pressed.

"She can't ask that," the director snapped.

"This was supposed to be scripted questions only," Imelda pointed out.

A commotion at the door and the interviewer's loud complaints about being removed forced Ryan to his feet.

Security hustled the interviewer and the cameraman out. Then another team removed Imelda. Then it was just himself, and a frustrated Kaden left in the room.

"Do you know how much I want to answer that?" Ryan asked softly. "I'm sick of it hanging over me." He felt exposed as Kaden gripped his hands and looked into his eyes.

"Not now," he murmured. "Let's talk to your sister and your agent, but we're not explaining this without thinking it through."

"We're? There isn't a *we*. This was *my* fuckup. I didn't share the video, but they were my words."

Kaden tugged him to the door. "Let's go." He led Ryan through the path of reporters, fellow actors, and security staff, and Ryan attempted to act as if nothing was wrong. Imelda caught them as they reached the front door, pulling herself free from security with an irritated huff.

"Are you okay?" she asked Ryan.

"I'm good."

She patted his hand, and then Kaden got him out to the back of the hotel and out of the service entrance. They were in the car and away from there within ten minutes of the woman asking the one question everyone wanted an answer to.

"Do you think I should admit what I did, tell people why I said what I said. Open myself up?"

Kaden assessed him steadily. "If that was what you wanted, you would have done it by now."

"But Luke is where I was, and it's my responsibility to at least say something to him." Ryan slumped into his seat and scrubbed at his eyes. "He said he was in love with Paul, that he tried hard to make him happy, that he was convinced that if only I left them alone, everything would be okay. But I'm not the one who's done anything."

"Talk to Luke, try to make him see…"

"If he's like me, then he won't care. He'll be blinded by this rich guy with all the moves. He will have been told he's lucky that Paul is part of his life. He'll be told he's shit in bed and that no one else will want him. He's me."

"Then we'll find Luke and talk to him, together, but you need to stay away from Paul."

"I have something to tell you." Ryan bit his lip, regretting not telling Kaden immediately. "Paul messaged me, said if he could help me in any way, then he was there if I needed him. What if I talk to him? I could get him to see what he's doing to Luke."

"What did the messages say?" Kaden asked, and his tone was insistent as if he wasn't going to go away without an answer.

"Nothing important—"

"Let me read them, Ryan."

"There's nothing in them that is like the old Paul," Ryan explained. "He's agreeable and supportive and says he wants me back in his life. Maybe he's changed, I don't know. Maybe he and Luke have an open relationship."

Kaden gripped Ryan's arms and shook him a little. "Snap out of it," he ordered.

"What?"

"Listen to yourself."

Ryan blinked up at Kaden's face, seeing his hazel eyes wide with horror. What did Kaden mean? Snap out of what?

*All I'm doing is thinking that Paul isn't so bad and that he can help me—*

"Shit. What am I doing? See how easy it is for me to fall down the rabbit hole."

Kaden pulled him in close for a hug.

"I wouldn't have let you fall," he murmured.

Ryan held on tight and knew three things for sure— he could trust Kaden, he needed to stay away from Paul, but most all, he had to save Luke from himself.

*No.* Ryan flicked his thumb over the screen of his cell phone. *No.* He stopped, leaned close, and examined the profile picture. *Not him.*

The events of today had stirred his emotions into a dense, murky mess. He wasn't sure how he'd gotten through dinner with Imelda and the others and was glad to be back at the beach house.

*Damn that interviewer.*

Where Paul and the video were concerned, Ryan, with Carmen's and his agent's guidance, had reacted in a way that was for his self-interest, that was best for his peace of mind, his future, and the least messy way to avoid dredging up a past he couldn't help but feel ashamed about.

*It's not my fault.* Easy to say, harder to believe, despite the counseling.

His actions had been about defense, not offense. If he hadn't seen Luke with Paul at the party that night, the interviewer's question would still have stung, but it would have been easier to handle. He could have hit repeat on the tried and tested method of retreating into himself, keeping his head down until Carmen dragged him out to shake stern words of encouragement into him.

Things had changed the minute Ryan had laid eyes on Luke. He could no longer fool himself into thinking it was over because *he* had escaped Paul and the man's emotional manipulation. *I was naïve, ignorant, selfish.* He hadn't considered, hadn't wanted to—about what came next. About *who* came next.

It wasn't just about him anymore.

*Luke Hart.* Ryan tapped the screen over the *See More* prompt and the list of profiles expanded. *I'll never find him.*

There was a splash, and Ryan jerked his leg when Kaden grabbed his ankle. "Don't scare me like that." He was sitting on the side of the hot tub with his legs in the water, had been for nearly thirty minutes, Carmen on a sun chair next to him. With a sigh, he gripped the side with his free hand and held his cell to his chest. "What if I'd dropped my phone?"

Kaden knelt up in the water and placed his hands either side of Ryan. "You'll make yourself crazy," he said and rested his chin on Ryan's knee.

"Don't you mean crazier?" Ryan gave a humorless laugh. "I just thought…"

What had he thought? Luke didn't even appear on any of Paul's social media, but then again, if Luke was a secret, he wouldn't. What did he think searching social media sites for Luke's profiles would achieve? Give him proof, maybe? But evidence of what? That he was right and Luke was going through the same type of hell he had, possibly worse? Or just perhaps, he wanted to be proved wrong.

Neither option lightened his heart. Either Luke, a man Ryan had once called a friend, was suffering, or… he wasn't.

Ryan's throat tightened. And what if Luke wasn't, and he and Paul were fine, normal? Had Ryan just been projecting himself onto Luke? Did that mean… the things Paul had done, were they Ryan's fault after all?

"You okay?" Kaden's voice was calm, and in turn, it calmed Ryan.

He cleared his throat, turned back from the negative path his mind was sending him down. "Apparently, there's more than a couple of Luke Harts online."

Kaden pushed himself back, displacing the water as he moved to the other side of the tub. "Wow. Go figure."

He pursed his lips and met Kaden's gaze. "I know. Stupid, huh?"

"Not stupid." Kaden dipped lower, so the water covered his shoulders.

Ryan glanced at his phone then behind him. "I should leave it to Carmen, shouldn't I?"

His sister stood straight up, "Challenge accepted." She clutched her purse to her chest.

"What? Right now?"

"Of course right now. Plus Larry's here to take me back to the hotel."

As if on cue a car horn sounded.

"I'll let you know if I find anything." She hooked her hand round the back of his head as she passed, planting a firm kiss on his cheek. "Night." She squeezed his neck. "You too, Kaden. See you in the morning."

Kaden didn't say anything, only raised his eyebrows and smiled.

"Take care, sis." Ryan leaned back, watched Carmen through the house.

The ocean was just audible over the hum of the hot

tub, and a breeze blew past him. There was nothing he could do for the time being.

"Hey," Kaden said and was in front of him again. He covered Ryan's hand with his own. "Are you going to join me properly?"

They were alone now.

The sun was disappearing beneath the horizon, casting a yellow-purple haze through the layer of patchy clouds and across the water. Tonight was their last night at the beach house. Tomorrow they would relocate to a hotel in advance of the premiere.

Ryan shook his head. Tonight should be about him and Kaden. "You're right."

"What?"

"Nothing." Ryan leaned back and dropped his phone onto the folded towel on the nearest of the chairs. As Kaden moved back, Ryan got into the water. He edged toward Kaden, coming to kneel across his legs. Time to focus on the present. "I'm going to miss this place." He traced between droplets across Kaden's collarbone and shoulder.

"Are you looking forward to tomorrow night?"

Ryan sat back. "I don't know. Can I tell you tomorrow?"

Kaden nodded. He reached up, gently cupping Ryan's face, and encouraged him to lean down. They kissed, and then whatever cycle the hot tub was on came to an abrupt stop, and silence fell around them.

There was the sound of waves, an airy *whoosh* surrounding them as seagulls cawed somewhere in the distance.

The surface of the water rippled as Kaden lifted Ryan higher, and it was then Ryan became aware of

Kaden's erection. "Enjoying yourself?" He chuckled then gripped Kaden's shoulders and teasingly bounced over his lap, causing small waves to hit Kaden's chest.

"That's cruel."

Ryan crossed his wrists behind Kaden's neck and hugged him close. Beyond them, the evening light was fading. He leaned his head to Kaden's, his cheek brushing Kaden's ear. "You'll probably think this sounds cheesy, but… these last few days, despite the crap, I think it's the first time in a while I've felt…" He closed his eyes. "Happy."

He smiled when Kaden wrapped his arms around him. Kaden's hold was warm and wet, and the thought of their time together coming to an end stirred an ache in his heart. What happened next beyond their contracted relationship was a conversation they needed to have.

"That makes two of us," Kaden said and loosened his hold.

Ryan opened his eyes. "Kaden," he mumbled, his lips pressed to Kaden's hair. Kaden had one of his hands between them. Ryan rotated his hips, biting down on his lip as Kaden slipped his fingers up the leg of his shorts to brush the base of his hardening dick.

"I know I said to join me, but…" Kaden turned his head, grazed kisses along Ryan's jaw. He held Ryan's face, nudged their noses together before pushing his mouth to Ryan's.

"We should go inside." Ryan's whole body ached for Kaden.

"We should."

Together they stood, the level of the water dropping. Quickly, they left the hot tub, wrapped themselves in the crisp white robes, kicking off their wet shorts onto the decking, then headed inside. Kaden drew the drapes, secured their privacy, a moment solely for them.

What happened then was a fumble of passion and desperation. They came together with quick kisses and touches, pushing each other's robes back as Kaden guided Ryan toward the sofa. They dropped onto the seat, and then it was all about the realization of release. Hands, mouths, their lower bodies rutting together. The heat of excitement washed over Ryan in strong waves, pushing him toward a climax.

"Fuck." He came, followed by Kaden, and exhausted, they slumped together.

Kaden breathed heavily, groaning as he tried to peel their damp bodies apart. The scent of the water's chemicals clung to their skin. "Okay, so that happened."

Ryan laughed and draped his arm over his eyes. He smiled when Kaden pressed a kiss to his chest.

"I'm going to clean up. Do you want to go back out?" Kaden asked.

Ryan rolled his head and stared at the drapes covering the door. "I think I'm done, but if you want to, I don't mind sitting out on the deck, keep you company."

"I'm good. I'll grab a shower, then cover the tub." He leaned down, kissed Ryan slow and tender. "Back soon."

"Okay." He needed to move.

After mustering the energy, Ryan left the sofa. It didn't take him long before he was back, curled in the corner in shorts and his hooded sweater. He was tired after an eventful day. The message tone of his cell *pinged*, and Ryan pulled it from his pocket. It was from Carmen.

He let out a heavy breath as he read the start of her message.

*Found him.*

Luke had been easy enough to track down or at least easy enough for Carmen to locate. How she'd done it, Ryan didn't know, but the coffee shop was out of the way, and he was supposed to be meeting Luke there at ten. They were leaving for the city today, ready for tonight's premiere, but right now, all he needed to do was to talk to Luke, get him to see that he was here for him.

"Are you sure about this?" Kaden asked, blatantly unhappy with what Ryan was doing. They'd been dropped off around the corner, and thirty minutes early for the meet and now sat on the wall at the edge of the parking area, out of sight.

"We used to be friends, okay? And maybe Paul *is* different with Luke, but what I saw in Luke's eyes, Kaden, it was a vicious pain, and I know what that is like."

Kaden took Ryan's hand, and they sat in silence, Ryan's breath hitching every time someone approached the café.

Finally, a gray sedan pulled up near the door and parked, but it wasn't Luke who climbed out. It was Paul.

Paul, who shielded his eyes from the sun and peered into the café.

"He found out and wouldn't let Luke come," Ryan said and pressed his free hand to his chest.

"Maybe that's his first mistake? Maybe Luke will see him for what he is," Kaden murmured and squeezed his hand. They slipped off the wall and left the parking area by the back gate, making their way through the side roads to the place where the driver had parked. Only when he was back in the safety of the car did Ryan slump miserably to one side.

This time, though, he didn't force himself into the corner.

He curled into Kaden.

And he felt as if nothing could hurt him.

## Chapter Thirteen

"Over here. Ryan. Ryan. If you can look this way, Ryan?" The voices of the photographers merged into one long string, accompanying the flashes from their cameras as they tried to get a shot of Ryan staring in their direction.

The whole event was overwhelming. So many lights, so much sound, so many people. This was a whole other world as far as Kaden was concerned, and he felt out of place.

Kaden glanced over his shoulder to where Carmen was watching over them. As soon as they'd stepped out of the car, Carmen seemed to have switched to assistant mode. She kept herself at a suitable distance until it was time to guide Ryan to where he needed to be, helping him traverse the array of cameras and mic-holding interviewers lining the walk to the entrance, able to prioritize those who were low risk, who would ask the *right* questions.

Kaden had stayed at his side, looking on adoringly as Ryan spoke, gentle touches to his chest or shoulder, joining in when he laughed. Ryan was amazing, his words as perfect as the outfit he'd chosen for the evening, a tailored gray suit over a black shirt and black paisley tie.

They walked hand in hand to the entrance, a brief moment to breathe before facing the line of cameras in front of a backdrop of the movie's logo.

After a few shots as a couple, Kaden faded into the background for a while, watching as Ryan posed solo, then mingled with others from the main cast for group shots.

"Go ahead," Carmen said and nudged him in the small of his back. The photographs were over, and it was time to move on.

Ryan met his eyes and held his hand out for Kaden to join him. "Okay?" he mouthed as he took hold of Kaden.

With a nod, Kaden smiled, moving close enough for their shoulders to touch.

"Nearly there."

The evening moved in a blur of light and sound and faces. More talk, more pictures, Ryan's face emblazoned on a massive screen as they sat in darkness, his and Ryan's fingers laced together, and holding on to each other tightly. It was an experience like no other Kaden had ever had, never would have had if Ryan hadn't walked into Gideon's office.

At times as the movie played, Kaden turned away from the screen, settled his gaze on Ryan's dimly lit face. Ryan seemed happy, comfortable in himself, and that made Kaden's heart swell. But it also cast a cloud of doubt. Was it okay for him to be with someone like

Ryan? Was he allowed to imagine a future for them beyond their contracted time?

"I'm beat," Ryan said as they walked the corridor to their hotel room. He leaned his head on Kaden's shoulder. "I thought we'd never get away."

Kaden rested his hand on Ryan's waist and hugged him close. The after-party had been fun, and Kaden had felt good about seeing Ryan being able to enjoy himself, especially considering his failure to meet up with Luke that morning.

He looked down at Ryan. Now wasn't the time to bring it up, but he wondered what Ryan intended as a next step? Would he continue to seek Luke out? Now Ryan knew about him and Paul, he wasn't going to be able to forget.

"This is us."

Kaden swiped the keycard and pushed open the door. He was surprised when Ryan stepped in front of him, gripped his wrist, and pulled him into the room and a tight embrace.

Soft sounds fell from Ryan's lips as he pushed Kaden against the closed door, hungrily capturing his lips in an openmouthed kiss. When the pressure of his kiss lessened, Ryan rested his hands on Kaden's chest. Leaning back, he gave a heavy sigh. "Thank you for tonight. For all of it."

Kaden placed his hands over Ryan's. "I think you did most of it yourself." He kissed Ryan tenderly, drinking in every moment. His mind went to his earlier thoughts of *what next?*

Dare he ask? It turned out he didn't have to.

"So, what happens next?" Ryan said. "With us?"

"What do you want to happen?"

Ryan worried his lower lip. "Once you check out tomorrow, that's it. Contract ended. You fly back to New York, and it's back to reality."

Kaden squeezed Ryan's hands. But what came after? Kaden wanted to know as well. He'd enjoyed getting close to someone, had convinced himself he was ready to move forward, bare his heart if Ryan wanted to. "What do *you* want?" he said again, his voice low, calm.

"I think I want to try being me when I'm with somebody again." Ryan huffed a laugh. "Is that a contradiction?"

Kaden laughed. "I don't know. Maybe?" Were you every truly yourself when with someone else?

"What I meant was, with Paul, I slowly became less and less of myself. Friends became distant, my family too, though seemed it was impossible to shake Carmen. She is my PA, after all." He laughed, but it was a laugh of sadness, regret. "As the relationship went on, I didn't dress like me, act like me, go places or do the things I wanted to do." He leaned forward, rested his forehead against Kaden's chest. "I want to know what it's like, who I am when it's a good relationship. An equal one."

A weighty pressure gripped Kaden's heart. They didn't know each other that well, and yet Ryan was willing to believe in him. He'd been concerned about Ryan hurting him, but what if it turned out he was the one who would end up dicking Ryan over? Was that genetic?

"Are you okay?" Ryan asked.

"What? Yes."

"Really?"

Kaden shrugged. "I think so." He met Ryan's curious eyes, then looked up at the ceiling. "Sorry."

"Burned."

"What?"

"You said you'd been burned in the past."

Kaden raised an eyebrow as he thought back. "Oh, you remember that."

"I do." Ryan made a fist. "And I want to ask about it, ask about the who, the how, if you're still hurting." He tapped his closed hand against Kaden's chest. "If being with me makes it hurt more?"

"I don't think now is the right time to talk about all that. It's long and complicated and you have enough going on without juggling my baggage." It looked like Ryan was going to argue, so Kaden quickly added, "But that last part I will answer, because that's easy." He wrapped his hand around Ryan's and firmly said, "No."

Ryan slowly relaxed his fist, allowing Kaden's fingers to lace though his.

"It's the opposite, in fact. Being with you is warm, comfortable, and makes me smile. You make me happy." He ducked his head, met Ryan's mouth in a tender kiss.

"Then…" Ryan looked hopeful.

"What I'm scared of is me messing things up. You're dealing with a lot at the moment and you're making steps to move on with your life. I don't want to get in the way of that."

Ryan shook his head. "I trust you."

"You do?"

"Yes. And I want you to be able to do the same, to be able to tell me stuff, to let me close."

"Thank you."

"For what?"

"For trusting me." He considered his next words. "In which case, I need you to trust me now. I'm about to suggest something, so don't think I'm not interested in this thing we've got going on, but…"

Ryan's brow creased.

"Hey, I said don't think. Just hear me out."

"Okay," Ryan said.

"As you said, I'm supposed to go back to New York tomorrow, and you'll be doing whatever it is a Hollywood star does with his weekend. I think that's a good thing. We've been thrown into this situation, you especially, when there's all this"—he raised his hands and held them either side of his head, curled his fingers like claws—"chaos about us."

Some time apart would give them both a chance to think on things, about their feelings toward themselves and each other.

"Are you about to give me the line from *Speed?*"

"*Speed?* Oh, the movie." He laughed and the air around them seemed less dense. "I guess that's kind of where I'm going."

"Okay," Ryan said again. "You make a good argument."

It was for Ryan as much as it was for himself. He liked Ryan, he liked being with him, but for both their sakes, he needed to back away so Ryan could understand his feelings.

"Right." Ryan tugged the collar of Kaden's jacket as he drew in a long breath. "That's enough serious talk." He pulled Kaden toward him, locked lips in a firm kiss, and pushed his thigh into the space between Kaden's legs, nudging his crotch.

Kaden's heart raced, pounded in his ears. Ryan was

sexy, serious, a bit pushy, and damn, it resonated with him.

When they parted, Ryan took him by the hand and said, "Let's take it to the bedroom."

Kaden loosened his tie and grinned. Whatever came after tomorrow, nothing was stopping them from being together right then. Briefly, he dragged Ryan back and stole a kiss. "Lead the way."

"Got everything?" Ryan asked as they waited for the elevator.

Kaden nodded. "Yes, thank you."

They were playing out their final scenes, a few hours together before a romantic farewell at the airport and public declarations they would see each other soon. But officially that was it, time up, job done and paid for. He checked around them.

Ryan closed the space between them and smiled. "So what's next for you?"

"Me?" Kaden blew out. "I'll need to check formally with Gideon, but after that… no idea. I don't have anything lined up, so I guess I'll focus on my other job."

"You have another job?"

"Kind of."

Ryan leaned his head. "Is this a plot twist?" He chuckled.

"Nothing that exciting." The elevator doors opened. There were others already riding the car. "Another time," he said and stepped in. The button for the ground floor was already lit.

The ride down was filled with an awkward silence, and Kaden was relieved when the doors opened, and he was greeted with the open space of the reception area. He yawned. "Man, I think last night is catching up with me." He blinked and looked at Ryan, who wore a strange expression. The color seemed to drain from his face as he hugged his waist.

"What's wrong?" Kaden turned around, following Ryan's gaze to where Luke was standing against a pillar. "That's…"

Luke checked over his shoulder, then stepped forward. He was wearing jeans and a loose-fitting woolen sweater, his features were sullen, and he winced as he tongued his split, swollen lip. He stopped in front of them.

"Hi," he said and pushed his hands into his pockets, dropped his shoulders. He eyed Kaden, then focused on Ryan. "I know I have no right to ask this, but…" He took a breath, straightened his back, then said, "Please. Can we talk?"

## Chapter Fourteen

Ryan glanced around him, trying to find somewhere private, desperate to grab and hold on to Luke before his friend ran. The nearest door, to the Lester Suite, was ajar, and holding out his hand to Luke, he inclined his head that way.

"Of course."

The room was empty of staff, set up with banks of chairs and a big screen at the front, ready for a meeting, although there were no signs indicating that they would be inundated with people in the next few minutes. This was about as private as they could get without renting a room for another night.

With a hand on the small of Luke's back, Ryan encouraged him to a chair, and he sat, then stood up again and began pacing. Kaden moved to stand in front of the door, probably thinking, like Ryan, that he would leave before he said what he'd come to say.

Was this going to be more criticism of what Ryan was doing? Of how he was messing up what Luke and Paul had going on? Or was the expression of defeat on

Luke's face an indication that he was desperate and searching for help? Ryan wished he could read into Luke's closed expression, but his old friend was giving nothing away. He was agitated and limping now, and finally, he stopped pacing and slumped into the nearest seat.

Ryan sat opposite him, carefully examining and listing the wounds he could see this close. The cut on Luke's lip was visible, there was bruising on one temple, and he seemed exhausted.

"Do you need a doctor?" he asked.

"No."

"Okay, but I think you should have someone take a look at—"

"No. I'm fine. Let me say what I need to say, please."

Luke was tense, anxious, and looked as if he was ready to run, possibly back to Paul. Ryan knew from firsthand experience that never ended well.

"Can we do anything to help?" Kaden prompted.

Luke tilted his chin. "Yes. No. I don't know." He winced as he spoke, the answers pulled from deep inside him where Ryan imagined the pain had been hidden for a long time.

"What happened, Luke?" Ryan braced himself, not entirely ready to hear the answer.

"You did," Luke said, his voice cracking on the second word. He coughed to cover it and wouldn't meet Ryan's eyes, but the passion in the words was enough for Ryan to know he was angry. "*You* were the one who made this happen."

Kaden left his place by the door and pulled up a chair, close enough to Ryan that he could if he wanted, reach out to hold his hand. This sounded like it was going to be another lecture about everything that was Ryan's fault.

*I wish I could hold Kaden's hand.*

"You want to explain that statement more?" he prompted, and Luke startled as if he wasn't even aware of what he'd just said.

"What?"

"You said it was my fault."

"Oh, yeah. I mean, last night, he saw... the two of you at the premiere, and he didn't like it."

Ryan tensed. He knew what happened when Paul didn't like something. At first, it would be words, cutting hurtful digs, accusations flying, but it didn't stop there, often ending in angry sex that hurt more than words ever could. Was that why Luke had a split lip? Paul had never cut Ryan where it would show on camera, and had never gone this far with him.

"Did he do that to you?"

"What?"

Luke appeared disconnected from what he was saying, his expression altering from defiance to desolation in an instant.

"Your lip? Did he hit you?"

"This?" Luke touched his lip and winced. It was a deep split and had to hurt like a bitch. "No, believe it or not, I caught it on the headboard of our bed. He didn't hit me. At least not there." He huffed a laugh, humorless and brittle, and then in a smooth movement, he lifted his T-shirt. Red marks covered his belly, but Ryan didn't get a chance to catalog it all before Luke dropped his shirt. "The hitting was everywhere else."

He closed his eyes again, and the effort to speak was obvious.

"Do you need to go to the hospital? Do you want me to call a cab?" Kaden asked. He pulled his cell out even as he asked, but Ryan shook his head subtly. Luke was right on the edge of something here, a realization of sorts, an epiphany maybe. "He might have internal bleeding," Kaden warned.

"I already said I'm fine," Luke snapped, his eyes wide. "If you must know, I went there this morning. So please, just let me talk."

Kaden leaned forward, saying, "Really?"

Luke stared right at Kaden, and there was momentary defiance in his expression before it vanished in an instant, and he nodded. "Yes," he murmured, then subsided into silence, coughing to clear his throat. "After… When I woke up, I walked. He was asleep, and everything hurt, and I…"

"It's okay," Ryan comforted. "So, last night?"

"Last night was okay, but then he wanted… so the sex was…" He glanced at Kaden with a pained expression. "Y'know," he finished.

Ryan remembered the kind of sex that Paul wanted when he was pissed off, angry, demanding, demeaning. It was the worst kind of connection, and there was nothing resembling informed consent involved in any of it. Paul demanded and took until the other person gave in. Or at least that was how it had been for him when they'd been together. Seeing Luke now, Ryan doubted Paul had changed all that much.

"I know," he murmured, feeling awkward about what blanks Kaden might be filling in right now. Later, he would have to be honest with Kaden if there was any chance of them being together after this. For now, their relationship had been something to while away the time in among the madness.

*He's going back to New York. He* is *nothing more than a distraction, a temporary employee.* Ryan's chest tightened, and he glanced left at Kaden, meeting his troubled hazel gaze. He didn't want the spark of possibility to go out.

"It was the images, though," Luke continued. "The ones on the red carpet, the Getty ones, they were…" Luke rubbed his hands on his jeans and coughed. "You and Kaden looked so happy together, like you were meant to be next to each other, and Paul…" Luke stopped talking, his emotions seemingly getting the better of him, and he bent his head to compose himself. Ryan gave him some time to think, to get himself back to a point where he could talk. "I know he didn't mean it; he was just angry, and the photos were…"

Ryan knew where this was going. The adrenalin that had driven Luke to ask for help was subsiding until the anger and pain would become nothing but unwanted memories. He knew because this was the way Paul had manipulated him.

Temper flooded Ryan. "So he got angry that there were photos of an ex who should mean nothing to him, and he took that out on the man he's supposed to be with, by what? Is he forcing sex on you? Then, what? Hitting you? Hurting you? Did he threaten you? Did he refuse to listen to you? Did he rape you?"

"Ryan—" Kaden warned, but Ryan didn't hold back. Fire and passion for justice was the only thing that would break this cycle for Luke and stop him from retreating into a place where he took all the blame for himself.

Ryan pressed ahead. "Did he tell you that you were

worthless, that you meant nothing to him? Did he hold you down? Luke, look at me."

Luke glanced up, his eyes bright with anger and tears. "Don't you fucking talk about what he did. It was all your fault that—"

"That what? Is it my fault I've found a way to move on, that I was able to fall in love with someone else? Is that really my fault? Do you know why I left him? He hurt me, physically and emotionally. Bit by bit, he was controlling me more, and it was only because I got a part in the first movie that I even got away from him. That time out of his reach helped me wake up to what he was doing."

"Whatever, Ryan—"

"Don't you remember the night of the video? You were there with me. Have you watched what I said on there? How I threatened to out him to the entire goddamned world so that he'd finally admit he loved me? He was never going to love me, and don't you recall there was more to that video?" Ryan's chest tightened as he spoke, knowing that once Kaden heard this, there would be no going back. "I talked to you about how he could never love me, that he scared me, that I couldn't see a way out."

"You were drunk—"

"That was about the only time I had any courage," Ryan snapped. "You were there, taking photos of me, handing me beers. Jesus, you know all of this. You *know* what a fucking bastard he is. Why would you go with him?"

"That's not my fault!" Luke shouted, and Ryan realized that he'd gone too far when Luke stood, his hands in fists, temper crackling around him. Ryan stood just as quickly.

"I'm sorry, Luke. Shit, I didn't mean to say that. I know what he is like."

They remained in this face-off for a few moments, and then just as quickly, Luke collapsed in on himself, in tears, his arms wrapped around his waist as he sobbed.

*Fuck. All I did was dump my pain onto him.*

Ryan moved immediately to pull Luke in tight, holding him as he cried, tears in his own eyes as emotions rushed through him. Despair for Luke, guilt for shouting, hate for Paul. A staff member came into the room and then froze, but Kaden took care of it, ushering them out and then locking the door. The last thing that Luke needed was for a bunch of witnesses to be standing in a circle around him.

"You're so brave," Ryan said, over and over. "We can do this together. I'm here for you." *I'm here for you.*

How long they stood there, Ryan didn't know. All he did know was that Kaden didn't move, a welcome and settling presence just far enough away to give Luke privacy but near enough that Ryan could reach for him if he wanted.

"I want to tell someone," Luke said, gripping Ryan hard. "I need to tell people what he did. I have to be the last." He extricated himself from Ryan's hold and stepped away, lifting his chin, pulling back his shoulders, his eyes red from crying, and blood running from the cut on his lip that he'd opened up again. "I'm going to the police."

Dread consumed Ryan in an instant. If the authorities had this on record, if there was something tangible that the public could grab hold on to and connect to Ryan, then he wouldn't be Ryan, actor; he would be Ryan, victim.

What would that do to his career? He wasn't the guy who played sensitive parts. He was supposed to be the hero in these movies. The studio might drop him if he showed weakness of any kind.

"Ryan?" Kaden asked.

"What?" Ryan stared at his lover and knew what Kaden was asking. *Are you going with him? What will you do? What can I do to help you?*

Kaden gave a subtle shake of his head as if he didn't know what to say next. Someone needed to tell Ryan what to do because the weight of what he did now was too much to hold himself.

"It's not just me," he whispered. "These films support an entire force of people. If I make a fuss…"

Luke smiled at him, even though it didn't quite reach his eyes.

"I'm not asking you to do this with me, Ryan. Your secrets are safe with me now."

"Fuck. It was you who released the recording," Kaden accused, the first time he'd talked in a while.

"No. Jesus. It wasn't me." Luke's voice was filled with horror. "I kept it, and I shouldn't have, but maybe I needed to remind myself—I shouldn't have kept it. I'm sorry, Ryan. I understand if you…"

"That recording nearly destroyed my career and could have ruined my entire life."

*Where is this coming from? This isn't me.*

"No, it was Paul who put it out there," Luke murmured. "But I'm going to be honest and say he beat me to it. I would have done anything to tarnish you in his eyes. Paul wouldn't let me leave, and he hurt me. I just wanted him to love me, and I was so desperate that I would have released it if I'd thought it would help. What kind of a man does that make me?"

"What do you want me to do now?" Ryan asked, so many emotions whirling inside him; he didn't know how to corral any single one of them long enough to deal with it.

"Nothing," Luke said and held up a hand. "I'm doing what's right for me."

"You'll go on record that he abused you? You'll take it as far as you can go, to court if you could?"

Luke hugged Ryan, then moved back and gave a final nod. Shoulders back, he smiled again. "All the way."

"Me too," Ryan said with renewed determination.

"What?" Luke's eyes were wide. "You have the movie to think about—"

"I'm ready to do this," Ryan interrupted. "You see, I thought it was just me. I always thought he was obsessed with me, and it only happened because I was so young. But if I'd said something before, then you wouldn't be here—"

"No, you don't get to say that. I knew what he was like. You told me that night. I recorded you saying…" He stopped talking.

He wasn't making a lot of sense as he spoke, but Ryan heard the admission and the apology, none of which mattered. He wasn't thinking about the video or who'd recorded him or the words he'd said or even that Paul had released part of the recording. No, what he really wanted was for Luke to keep this determination and for the two of them to report what was happening.

"Paul wanted me vulnerable so that I would accept his offered help. No one else should be hurt."

"It was always about you," Luke murmured. "He wanted you back; he never wanted me."

"This won't be easy," Ryan warned. "He's a vindictive man, and we have a lot to lose. But together…"

Luke held out a hand to Ryan, but Ryan ignored it and instead pulled him in for another hug.

"Let's do this, Luke. Together."

## Chapter Fifteen

Kaden chewed on his thumbnail and stared out the passenger window of the taxi. Ryan was sitting beside him in the middle of the backseat, Luke on the far side. Who knew what was going through their heads right now?

"What about your flight?" Ryan said, breaking the silence. "Are you sure you shouldn't—?"

"As I told you, I'm staying." Kaden rolled his head, looked at Ryan, then beyond him to where Luke sat, pale, swallowing hard, restless. "There'll be other flights," he said. *But what you're doing needs to happen now. Maybe, finally, put an end to it.*

"Thanks." Ryan slumped and closed his eyes. The atmosphere in the car was tense, the new silence oppressive, but there had been something in Ryan's eyes. A glimmer of hope.

It wasn't long before they were piling out of the taxi around the corner from the police station.

"Thank you," Kaden said and paid the fare. He

waited for the car to pull away, then turned. Ryan and Luke were standing in the shadow of the building.

"I don't think I can." Luke clutched the neck of his sweater.

Ryan shook his head. "Of course you can."

"What if they don't believe me?" His breathing was uneven. "Or worse, what if they do?"

"How's that worse?" Ryan touched Luke's elbow.

"They believe me, they bring him in, talk to him, but then… he gets away with it. You remember who his family is, right? I can't fight that."

"I know it's scary." Ryan held up his hand, and Kaden noted the slight sway of his fingers. "I'm terrified." He made a fist. "But I meant what I said earlier. You are brave, stronger than you realize. Stronger than I ever was."

It was Luke's turn to shake his head. "You left before things got this bad. Me, I'm an idiot."

Ryan closed his eyes. "You're not. Neither of us was." He raised his head and looked firmly at Luke. "It messes with your head, that's all. His words, his actions. One minute you're in love and everything is perfect; the next there's this venom, this hate for him, but before you know it, he's apologized, or you find yourself apologizing as everything's twisted and somehow you're the bad guy, so he forgives you, you forgive him, and it starts all over again."

With a sigh, Luke leaned against the sizeable sand-colored stonework. "I could walk away as you did. Go back home."

"You could."

"Do you think my parents would forgive me?"

"For what?"

"For everything."

Kaden kept his distance. Ryan had mentioned before how his relationship with Paul had created a void between himself and his friends and family. Kaden imagined the same had happened to Luke, making an already stressful situation even harder to escape from. There would be nobody left to turn to for help.

"I do, and if that's what you want, I'll do anything in my power to help you." Ryan stopped, but it was clear from his tone there was a *but* to his proposal.

Luke understood. "But what then?" He gave a small smile. "Or *who*, right? Paul could do it again to someone else." He pushed off the wall, then folded his arms across his chest, the corners of his mouth curling downward as he asked, "Do you think he ever loved me?"

"I wish I could tell you he did, but..." Ryan shrugged. "I don't know."

Inhaling a deep breath, Luke straightened his back. "I figured as much." He stepped forward into the strip of sunlight illuminating the far side of the sidewalk as it shone from around the corner of the building. "Let's go inside before I talk myself in any more circles." His laugh was humorless.

"Okay." Ryan stood at his side.

"What are you doing here?" All three men turned to see a furious Paul stalking toward them. "Luke, get into the fucking car."

"How did he know where you were?" Kaden snapped.

Luke paled, yanking his phone from his pocket. "He has this software to know where I am. I should have turned it off, deleted it——"

"Get into the fucking car!" he shouted and caused more than a few heads to turn, including two cops in uniform.

"No," Luke said, staying calm and focused. "I'm going inside, and I'm telling them everything."

"He's not going anywhere with you," Ryan snapped.

Paul rounded on him. "I'm not finished with you either," he said, right up in Ryan's face.

"You're done, Paul. Finished."

Paul moved so quickly Kaden barely registered the step, pushing Ryan against the wall, his arm across his throat.

"Get. Into the. Fucking car," he shouted back at Luke. Kaden reached them first, yanking to separate them, Luke a step after.

Paul cursed and shouted, Luke hit out, Kaden held tight, and then the cops were there, sorting through the muddle.

"Just a misunderstanding," Paul simpered and handed over his card to the cops. What did he think that was going to achieve?

"I have film," a short blonde woman said and waved her phone. "I'm a witness to what happened to Ryan Levesque," she added, nearly bouncing on her toes.

With everyone herded into the station, there was nothing more Kaden could do.

"If you can come with me." Cop two gestured for everyone to follow Cop one, who had a secure grip on the struggling Paul.

Ryan looked at Luke. "Ready?"

"Not really," Luke said.

Ryan took the first step. "Come on."

Kaden followed them to the corner. "I'll have to give a statement, but I'll be here when you're done."

Ryan stopped for a moment. "Could you do something for me?"

"Of course."

"Could you call Carmen and let her know what's going on?"

Kaden nodded. "Sure."

"Thanks," Ryan said. Then he and Luke continued forward.

Kaden watched them for a few steps before going with another cop to give his statement. It didn't take long, and he found himself back out on the street. *Ryan will be fine. Right?* He was happy to offer whatever support or comfort Ryan needed, but he was sure these first steps were ones Ryan needed to take for himself, allowing him to move forward.

*That's how I felt.* Kaden had suffered his mother's temper through his early teens. It had taken him a long time to realize that wasn't how a mom was supposed to be, eventually taking a chance on a teacher who'd been kind to him, asked her for help. That was when things had changed for him. He'd been sent to live with grandparents he'd never met, connected with family, including Gideon, he'd never known existed.

*Not everyone's an asshole.* He pulled out his phone and stared at the blank screen. He should get Carmen up to speed.

"Hello?" Carmen said when the call connected after the second ring.

"Hi," Kaden said. "Are you all right?"

Carmen laughed. "Kaden. Um, sure. Are you? Did you get to the airport okay? Forget something? Larry isn't back with Ryan yet, so haven't heard about how teary the farewell was."

"We never made it to the airport. Something came up. And sorry, I've no idea about Larry." They had chosen to take a cab downtown instead of waiting for Larry and the car to show up.

"What? Let me talk to Ryan."

"About that——"

"Where's Ryan? Did something happen? What's going on? Is he okay? And what do you mean you've no idea about Larry?" With each question, she became more frantic. "Put Ryan on now."

"Calm down," he said. "Ryan's fine. So please, calm down so I can tell you what's going on."

"Okay," she said, sounding calmer, just. "Start talking."

"Ryan is with Luke. He showed up at the hotel this morning, having taken a beating from Paul."

"Seriously?"

"Yes, I won't go into details over the phone, but the two of them are at the station right now talking to the cops. And Paul is here as well. He assaulted Ryan, and I don't know what else is going on."

"Seriously?" she said again, her voice louder, incredulous as it rose at the end of the word. "Okay. Oh, shit. Wait, as in Ryan's making a statement?"

"I believe so. He asked me to call you. I don't know who else needs to know, but they went in a few minutes ago."

Carmen fell into a short silence.

"Do you need me to do anything?"

"Erm, no. Right. Thanks. Actually, could you message me exactly where you are? My brain is a little overwhelmed right now, so I'm not sure I'd take it in if you told me. He just went in, right? So he'll be a while." She was moving around as she spoke. "Okay. I'll get hold of Larry. The moron's probably walking in circles around the hotel, hoping he doesn't have to tell me he lost you both. And then we'll be right over."

"I don't know if they'll let you collect it, but our luggage is being held by reception."

"Sure, I'll see what I can do. If you hear anything before I get there, call me. Otherwise, drop me that text, and I'll be there as soon as I can. Bye."

When Carmen hung up, Kaden let out a heavy breath and scratched the back of his neck. *I should contact Rowan.* He sent the details of the police station they were at to Carmen, then navigated his phone to make the call to Rowan.

"Kaden." Rowan's cheery voice was strangely comforting.

"Hey," Kaden said.

"I didn't expect to hear from you until tomorrow. Is everything okay?"

"Short answer, yes. Slightly longer answer, I won't be coming back to New York today, so could you find me a flight for tomorrow. Actually, make that in a couple of days?"

There was the sound of Rowan leaning back in his chair. "Okay," he said, his tone one of suspicion. "And the even longer answer? There is one I presume?"

Kaden eyed the people in the street. He probably shouldn't have been discussing the details out in public. "Can I get back to you on that? It's a personal matter Ryan is dealing with. I just didn't feel good about walking away right now."

"That's fine. I'll look into getting you a new flight and let you know the details once I do. You can update us when it's convenient and what, if any, role you or Bryant & Waites has in the situation."

"Thank you." Kaden rubbed at his eyes. "I'm sorry if I've dragged us into something." Paul's most recent actions were in part because of Kaden, because of the perceived relationship he'd been contracted to act out. He had no idea how far things would go once Ryan and Luke had made their statements to the police, but it could come out that Kaden had been hired to play a part, and if what Kaden knew of Paul was right, the man would find a way to twist it in his favor, make Ryan the bad guy again.

"I can hear the grinding."

"Hmm?"

"You're thinking too hard."

"Sorry."

Rowan sighed. "Don't worry about it. Do what you think is for the best. It'll work out somehow. For now, go be with Ryan. I'm sure he'll appreciate the support."

"Thanks. I'll be in touch soon."

"Take care."

"Bye." Kaden lowered his cell. He stared back along the street. *Ryan said he'd contact me when he was finished.* There was no point hanging around outside. He had no idea how long Ryan might be. *A cold drink would be good.* He'd find a café or somewhere to wait nearby.

Time seemed to stall, every minute passed slowly, but after a couple of hours, Ryan phoned and said they were done, and Kaden headed back to meet him.

"Hey," he said as he reached Ryan's side.

"Kaden." Ryan wrapped his arms around Kaden's

neck and buried his face in his shoulder. He let out a shaky breath.

Kaden embraced Ryan gently. "What happened with Paul?"

Carmen was on her phone, and Luke looked exhausted.

"They arrested him for assault, and that's enough for now," Ryan said. "He's in the system, and we've done what we could."

"The assault video is viral." Carmen sighed.

"I thought the woman gave the cops her phone?"

"This is LA. There are phones everywhere. I've made a simple statement and tweeted it, but we need to look at the bigger picture on social media, and the studio is trying to get hold of us."

Ryan buried himself in Kaden's hold, and Kaden was happy to block out the world for him, if only for a few minutes. "You did good," he said and pressed a kiss into Ryan's hair.

"Maybe," Ryan mumbled. "But it's done." He inhaled and leaned back. "I just want to go to the hotel and forget about everything for today." He took hold of Kaden's hand. "What about you? Are you getting a later flight? Or…" His grip tightened.

"It'll be tomorrow at the earliest now."

Ryan nodded, then checked out Luke. "Do you have anywhere to go? Anyone you can call?"

Luke pressed his palm to his forehead. He was pale. "I don't know. Maybe." He was lost, alone as he put distance between himself and the others. "I might have enough cash on me for a room somewhere. I don't have any bank cards on me. Paul usually found reasons to hold on to them."

It was Carmen who stepped toward him. She pressed her phone to her chest and rested her hand on his shoulder. "It doesn't matter. We were moving hotels anyway, and now that the premiere's over, you can come with us. We'll get you a room at the hotel. And if there isn't one I'm sure they can set up an extra cot in one of the rooms."

Though it seemed Luke wanted to argue at first, weariness clouded his expression, and he slumped but agreed. "Okay."

She returned to her phone call, giving a few more words and nods before she hung up. "Right. If you're not needed, let's get out of here."

Nobody was going to argue.

"I'll call Larry to bring the car around."

Ryan moved close to Kaden again, seeking more contact beyond their linked hands.

"It'll be okay," Kaden said, hooked a hand around the back of Ryan's neck, and pulled him to him.

"I hope so." Ryan's breaths were warm against his chest through the fabric of Kaden's T-shirt. "Thank you for today. And before you say you didn't do anything"— *How did he know?*—"just being here is enough."

Kaden rested his cheek on the top of Ryan's head. His heart swelled at the thought his presence meant so much to another person, to Ryan. He hugged Ryan. "You're welcome."

# Chapter Sixteen

Paul's arrest made the news in a big way, and when the informal statement Ryan had given made it online, the shit hit the fan, and opinions were divided. The ones who put two and two together and linked the angry video outburst with the fact that Ryan was proclaiming Me Too were mostly sympathetic. A lot of comments on Twitter were ones of admiration for him standing up, but there were a ton of retweets that accused him of cynically climbing onto the bandwagon to get movie sales. Others said that abuse didn't happen to men. Some said Ryan and Luke probably asked for it. Yet more shared their own stories.

He'd expected that. After all, he hadn't come forward any earlier, and because of that, he'd been complicit in the lies and in Paul being able to hurt Luke.

"Maybe we should have had a SAG rep in here with us." Arthur Dennis was there with him, and as Ryan's agent, he was caught between a rock and a hard place.

Ryan sighed. Union representation would mean an escalation he wanted to avoid.

"I said no."

"Fuck," Arthur cursed, which was a new thing because he didn't do that regularly. "I wish you'd spoken to me first," he insisted.

"You said that already." Ryan tried to stay patient with Arthur because this had been dropped unceremoniously onto his agent's head. Still, as an agent, he was flailing all over the place over this. Maybe it was time to get a new agent.

Today's studio meeting was the next step, and they were outside the head office, waiting for the more comprehensive reaction. Lawyers had already gone in, but as yet Ryan and Arthur hadn't been invited in. He didn't care what kind of lawyers they had on their side. He'd already decided he wouldn't fight the studio if they wanted to let him go, even if he'd done nothing wrong. He had other ideas about how he could work to spread the word about people like Paul, some of which he wanted to talk to Luke about.

His cell vibrated, and he checked the message immediately, a short expression of support from Kaden who'd decided he was coming to this meeting to sit outside in case Ryan needed him. Ryan wished, not for the first time that it was Kaden sitting next to him, with his unconditional support and love.

Love. How the hell had that happened? How was it that pretending to be in love had become so much more than that? *What happens when he goes back to New York? Will he still work as a boyfriend for hire?*

"I could have managed it, made it work for us, not against us," Arthur muttered. "You issued a fucking statement without me even seeing it."

Ryan had listened to this over and over, but

something in Arthur's expression and the muttered words made Ryan's temper flare. "This isn't something to be remade into positive PR; this is real fucking life."

Arthur subsided after glaring at Ryan, and there wasn't any more time to talk when the secretary announced that Abby Haynes would see them now. Ryan knocked, waited for the "come in," and shoulders back, he went in and offered the studio head his hand, aiming for an unconcerned expression.

"Ms. Haynes." He was polite and formal as he took the seat opposite her. One by one, the lawyers left, all four of them in gray suits and sporting serious expressions. Not one of them smiled. Not a single man there held back to give Ryan a thumbs-up.

The thought of one of them grinning and giving him two thumbs made Ryan feel lighter. If he lost his job, if he was blacklisted, if this was the end, then Carmen had been right. There was always the provincial theatre in Canada option.

"While we would have preferred a structured statement and prior knowledge of what happened, the studio would like to offer our full support for your situation."

Ryan blinked at her, waiting for the "but".

"And?" Arthur asked, clearly suspicious of such an easy acceptance.

Abby leaned forward, a sharp-dressed woman, with perfect makeup and an aura of authority.

"The Me Too movement is too important for anyone to stay quiet, Ryan. As of five p.m. tonight, the studio has cut ties with Paul Feldstone and his father's firm. The lawyers are on that as we speak. Now." She steepled her hands, and Ryan tensed. If she was going to fire a shot, he assumed it would be now. "I admire that you want to support Luke Hart, and I'd like us to work out the positive message we can create together."

This was the complete opposite of what Ryan had been expecting, so much so that he was lost for words, and it was up to Arthur to talk for him so they could leave. The longer it took, the weirder Ryan felt as the enormity of everything began to weigh him down. The office was claustrophobic, the air thin, and the collar of his shirt seemed too tight, and as soon as they were done, he rushed through the building to the rear exit and out the door into the hot and humid LA air. This was where Kaden would be waiting for him, and he headed straight over to the man staring down at his phone with a thoughtful expression. He must have sensed Ryan coming over, and he stood straight and smiled, opening his arms as Ryan flew into them and held on tight.

"What happened?" Kaden asked. "Do you need to get a lawyer—?"

"No, no…" Ryan burrowed into Kaden's hold. "They were supportive. It's fine."

Kaden eased him away and tipped Ryan's chin with a finger. "So why are you hugging me this hard?" He was so damned serious, searching for any lie that Ryan might be telling to keep him calm.

"I just needed a hug—the office was too small for me to pace."

Kaden pulled him close again. "I can hug."

They stood in silence for a while, then headed for the car and back to the hotel. Ryan wanted to spend whatever time they had left in bed or talking or anything but answering the calls that kept coming in. Carmen, the studio, Arthur, Imelda—everyone wanted to talk to him, and when Luke knocked on the door, Ryan gave up imagining that he and Kaden could have private time.

"I was thinking," Luke said, standing in the corridor and hovering. He was so uncertain, and Ryan opened the door wider and gestured him in. "No, I don't have to come in. I don't want to interrupt anything," he said.

"You're not disturbing me."

Luke stepped in and glanced around nervously. "If you're doing something with Kaden…"

"He's taking a shower," Ryan explained, trying not to dwell on the fact that he had been seconds away from surprising his lover and joining him. "You want coffee?"

"I don't want to be a bother…" Luke shook his head and scowled. "I need to stop apologizing."

Compassion welled inside Ryan. He knew what it was like to second-guess people's thoughts about you. Hell, he'd done it with Kaden all this time and still had small niggling doubts.

"It's natural," Ryan reassured. "It took me a while to get my head straight, and even then, it's not completely right."

Luke's shoulders fell, and he slumped onto the sofa. "What do I do?" he said and tossed the folder onto the small coffee table. "I'm in my room, thinking up all the kinds of things I can do to help others, and how can I even think of doing that when I'm so messed up?"

Ryan sat next to him, put an arm over his shoulders, the sound of the shower steady in the background.

"I'm telling you now everything will be okay," Ryan murmured. "You'll muddle through life, and you'll take positive steps and have bad days and good, and then you'll find people you love and maybe even a special guy, and everything will begin to make sense."

"Like you did, with Kaden."

Ryan huffed a soft laugh. "I'm still messing that up now. I want to ask Kaden to be with me, but what if he says no? What if he tells me that I'm not worth having to deal with all this mess?"

Luke shot him a look of disbelief. "Seriously? Anyone with eyes can see he's into you."

"I know, and I'm ready to believe I can have someone like him. I just need to talk to him, and that's what you'll do. You'll talk to people, and you'll see that not every partner is out to hurt you."

Luke nodded and wriggled away from Ryan's hold, picking up the folder. "A charity reached out to me, and… did you know I have a lawyer?"

That was a quick change in subject. "Okay?"

"I mean, not the kind of lawyer that needs to be paid for. This one works for the charity on pro bono cases. His name is Martin, and he's this hotshot attorney who represents all these big stars, and he's in my corner. He wants a meeting. Anyway, that is where the idea came in. The charity is offering me the chance to work with them, and it might be something good. You know?"

"May I see?"

He handed the folder over, and Ryan skimmed the information on the charity's aims.

"Keep me in the loop, right? I'll do what I can with them as well."

Luke's eyes widened. "Really?"

"It happened to me, too, and you're my friend. If working together means one person can get help, then we owe it to them. Also, we have an entire court case to get through at some point. We're going to need each other."

"Hi, Luke," Kaden said from the bedroom door, dressed, his hair damp.

"Hey," Luke said and ducked his head. "Anyway, I need to go. My mom and dad are arriving in an hour, and I want to get my head straight."

Ryan hugged him. "You know where we are if you need anything."

"He seems quiet," Kaden observed after he'd left.

"He is, but he'll be okay." Ryan was sure of it or at least he wouldn't let Luke be alone with everything he was going through.

Kaden pulled him close. "Missed you in the shower," he said between kisses. "It was lonely in that huge room without you. So I saved myself and thought we could say good-bye properly in the bedroom on a bed, in comfort, and *then* get another shower."

"I wish you could stay with me for all of this," Ryan blurted and edged away with a sudden unaccountable fear that he'd just fucked things up. Kaden had been teasing about saying good-bye, keeping things light, and Ryan had dumped a bucket load of serious onto his head.

"About that." Kaden took Ryan's hand and led him to the sofa. "I've been talking to Gideon. You know the guy who owns the agency?"

"Yeah?"

"He says that… look, I'll show you." Kaden pulled out his phone and tapped some buttons, and it was all Ryan could do to yank him close for more kisses. How can a man make scrolling on his phone sexy? He turned the cell, and Ryan winced at the photo. It was of the two of them after the night club visit with a lurid headline and an entire article dedicated to the man from New York who'd swept the actor off his feet.

"They're not wrong," Ryan said. "You did sweep me off my feet."

"Gideon is saying that work might not be easy now. Y'know. The pretend boyfriend thing."

"Shit." Ryan hadn't even thought about that. If they'd broken up publicly, as planned, and Kaden had gone home, then he wouldn't be the center of media attention, but now, he was in the middle of a court case, with repercussions neither of them could imagine.

"But it's okay. I have money saved, enough to take an extended break from the boyfriend business, and who knows, maybe find new work, set up my own company."

"A rival fake boyfriend company?" Ryan joked.

"No, for my real work. I test company security systems, maintain firewalls, some coding. Where you picked me up? That's the company I work for. Gideon pulled some favors, got me in with them because well, he's my cousin, and he's a good guy. Plus they threw in a great discount on the apartment."

Ryan felt his jaw drop. "For real?"

"Yeah, they gave me a good deal on the place."

"Not that part."

Kaden grinned. "So which part?"

"The part where you're an honest-to-goodness white-hat hacker? Oh, and the part where you're not really a fake boyfriend for hire?"

Kaden snorted. "I am. I've done a lot of work for Gideon. It's fun. Pays well. I get to travel, see things I normally wouldn't."

Ryan scrubbed at his eyes. "Okay, then."

"So, back to you not wanting me to go. Why don't you want me to go?"

"I thought that was obvious."

"Humor me."

"I love you, and as much as I want to get on a plane to New York right now, I guess I'm stuck here for a while until things die down."

Kaden took hold of his hand. "I wish I could stay longer. I mean, you've just told me you love me, and I want to be here for you, but I think it's for the best. For now, at least. You're needed here, and you're not alone."

"I know."

"Besides, it won't be forever, right? And it'll give us that space, a chance to reflect because I want to say it too."

Ryan looked up at him. "Say what?" He wanted to hear those words from Kaden.

"I love you. I want to be able to say it, and for you to know that I mean it."

"I want that." Ryan gripped Kaden's hand. He also wanted Kaden to believe in his words too. He thought back to the night of the premiere. "Will you tell me?"

"Tell you what?"

"About who burned you?"

Kaden leaned back. "You don't need to hear about that."

"Need? No. But I would like to." *I want you to trust me the way I trust you.* Was that selfish of him? "I feel like all you do is listen to my problems."

Kaden cleared his throat. "Well, they are very real and very present problems." He gently held Ryan's face, swept his thumb across his cheek.

Ryan looked into Kaden's eyes, hoped the expression

he wore was no longer the one of the angry, scared man he'd been when he'd walked into Gideon's office. He wanted to be someone Kaden could love and trust, share anything with.

"It was my parents," Kaden finally said. "My mother mostly."

"Parents?" Ryan glanced at the floor.

"What?"

"Sorry. I was just thinking how much harder it must be if it's family. I mean Paul was just…"

Kaden shook his head. "You loved him. Hurts all the same." He rubbed his hand over his hair. "My dad left when I was ten. Haven't seen him since."

"You don't know where he is?"

"No idea. I don't know if he's dead or alive, or has a new family. But he left and that meant it was just me and my mom." He sighed. "And as far as I was concerned she was all I had so I put up with a lot. Thought I had to."

"Did she hit you?"

"Sometimes. It was mostly shouting, blaming me for my dad leaving, but she'd push me, grab me by my hair, and..." Kaden fell silent and stared at the lamp across the room.

"You said Gideon was your cousin, right?" Ryan said. He wanted Kaden to keep talking.

Kaden's seemed to relax and Ryan felt as if his voice had shattered a blackness that had been sucking Kaden in.

"Yes. I found out about him when I was fourteen. Mom had never talked about us having any family. I always figured her parents, my grandparents, had passed away. Turned out they hadn't."

"How did you find them?"

Kaden blew out a steady breath. "As I got older I realized things weren't right at home. There was a teacher I had who was kind to me. I'm pretty sure I drove her insane at times, but she did what she could and seemed to be in my corner. I don't remember now what drove me to do it, but I eventually spoke up and asked for her help." He gave a sad smile. "Once the school got involved everything changed and I ended up being sent to live with my grandparents. Seemed they didn't know I existed either."

"For fourteen years?"

"Apparently. I don't know exactly what happened but they fell out over a man Mom was seeing at the time. My grandparents were good people, or were to me, so I don't know why but she cut them off completely, along with her two brothers." He bit on his thumbnail. "It's what she's good at. Once I was out of her life she didn't stick around for long. Disappeared the same as my dad."

Ryan gripped Kaden's hand. "I'm sorry."

"Family can be complicated." Kaden smiled a smile that chased the gray from his features. "And from what Rowan told me about your time on *Destiny Cove*, you'd know all about that."

Ryan laughed. "I guess."

"So that's the summary version." Kaden sat forward in a way that felt this was the period to end the conversation.

*For now at least.* Ryan wanted to know more, to know everything there was to know about Kaden, be it good, bad or painful. But he could wait. There would be other days. Even though they were going their separate ways for now, this wasn't the end.

"You'll let me know when you get back to New York?" Kaden said.

"God, yes." There were still things he had to do in LA before he could head back to his New York apartment.

"And maybe pick up from wherever we leave off tonight?"

As much as Kaden said about them needing some time apart, it felt like them, together, was already set in stone. "Definitely." The way Kaden looked at him made Ryan's heart swell. He wanted to be looked at that way forever.

"And obviously, I'd be looking to fill the position of an exclusive-going-everywhere-together boyfriend," Kaden said as he clambered to sit on Ryan's lap and pressed kisses to his face as if chasing away all the sadness and pain they shared.

"Everywhere together," Ryan repeated. "I could work with that."

"Then it's a deal."

A deal they sealed by making out on the sofa, taking it to bed, and *then* ending up in the shower.

# Epilogue

Kaden didn't want to open his eyes. He clung to sleep as he clung to the roll of the comforter that'd gathered in the center of the bed. He inhaled and exhaled, becoming aware of the presence that had disturbed his slumber as the mattress dipped.

He groaned and rolled onto his back as he felt fingers in his hair. "You're back," he said, smiling as he was greeted with a firm kiss.

"Miss me?" Ryan said and lay down beside him. He ran his hand over Kaden's chest.

"Nope," Kaden said.

"Not even a little?"

"Not at all." He laughed when Ryan prodded him. "Hey." He grabbed Ryan's wrist and pulled him close. "That tickles," he said, then nuzzled the side of Ryan's face, pressed kisses to his neck. He'd lied. He had missed Ryan, missed him every time he'd been away filming in the last two years.

Two years. Had it been that long already?

Ryan was warm and smelled good, and Kaden just wanted to curl up in the arms of his most important person. The one who was his everything, his comfort, his safety, his heart.

*I can't deny how good it feels to have him back. How it feels every single time.*

"What time is it?" Kaden uttered against Ryan's skin. He slipped his hand beneath Ryan's T-shirt and stroked a line across his stomach.

"Now who's tickling whom?" Ryan gripped Kaden's hand through the material.

Kaden opened his eyes, positioned himself to lean over Ryan. The glow of morning light filtered into the room from around the edges of the drapes. He blinked a few times, drank in the sight of his lover, his partner. "How was it going back to *Destiny Cove*?"

"Weird," Ryan said with a laugh. "So many new faces in the cast, and it made me feel old."

"Old? I've got two years on you, so you'd better not be saying you're old at twenty-six." Kaden curled his fingers, eliciting another laugh from Ryan and making him squirm.

"All right, all right." Ryan squeezed his hand tighter to stop Kaden's teasing touch. He rested his head on the pillow and sighed. "But it was fun being back on set. At times it was as if I'd never left. It was all so familiar and comfy."

Kaden stroked Ryan's bangs away from his face. "I'm glad it went well. You were on the show for—"

"Two and a half years," Ryan stated. He released Kaden's hand and raised both of them so they lay on his pillow either side of his head. "It was my first big role. I was eighteen and living the dream." He laughed.

The soap opera was celebrating its twentieth year on air and had brought back some of its most popular characters from over the years for a week of special episodes that would air in a couple of months.

"And then a handful of guest roles elsewhere and suddenly I'm signed onto the next big movie franchise. Well, what everyone hoped would be."

Kaden lifted his leg and straddled Ryan's thighs. He linked his fingers with Ryan's and pushed them down into the pillow. He leaned down and kissed him. "I really did miss you."

Ryan lifted his head and gazed at Kaden's crotch. "So it seems." He pushed into Kaden's hold. "I have way too many clothes on right now."

With a smile, Kaden shuffled back, then leaned down to nudge Ryan's T-shirt up with his nose. He nipped and sucked at Ryan's smooth stomach, working downward to tease the waistband of his pants with his teeth.

A needy groan tumbled from Ryan's parted lips as he arched his back.

"We should fix that," Kaden said. It had been over a week since he'd last been able to touch Ryan, and he had the strongest desire to claim him all over again. The same feeling he had every time Ryan returned to New York.

It didn't need to be said twice, and between fumbled tugs of clothing and awkward kisses, Ryan was stripped and the two of them finally naked together on the bed. Kaden hugged Ryan, caressing his heated skin as he pressed their erections together. Being held by Ryan had become his favorite thing in the world, the best sensation, the place he felt happiest as if they were untouchable.

"I love you," he mumbled.

"Same," Ryan said as he curled his fingers in the back of Kaden's hair, pulled his head back.

In those two years, Kaden had grown his hair back out, his curls brushing the tops of his ears as he arched his neck, allowing for Ryan to kiss him.

"Want me to show you?"

Ryan's words were like velvet to Kaden, and a strange sense of pride mixed with his excitement. Ryan's confidence in and out of the bedroom had bloomed during their relationship.

"Uh-huh." Kaden whimpered as Ryan kept his mouth just out of reach, his warm breath falling across Kaden's waiting lips.

Ryan smiled and leaned closer, the moment turning into one of hungry hands and openmouthed kisses, a whole lot of give and take.

After a brief break to grab supplies, they deepened their connection. Lube, fingers, pushing, stretching, and suddenly Ryan was sitting over him, easing his body down onto Kaden's waiting erection.

He gripped Ryan's hips, encouraged him lower until his ass was flush with Kaden's thighs. Kaden uttered words of desire as Ryan moved, desire for every part of him. Ryan pushed down. Kaden thrust up. The wave of motion continued over and over until Kaden was brought to a climax. He rode out his release, then wrapped his hand around Ryan's dick for a few short tugs until he reached his own orgasm, and he slumped forward, boneless, exhausted.

"I really do love you," Ryan said.

"I know."

Kaden stirred awake. He didn't remember when he'd fallen asleep but had done so while embraced by Ryan. He rolled over, surprised to find himself alone. He propped himself up on his elbows and eyed the crack in the door. With a sigh, he got to his feet, dressing in shorts and a T-shirt.

He brushed back his bangs and stepped out of the bedroom, squinting as he was met with a wall of light at the front of his apartment.

"Morning," Ryan said. He was sitting on the floor, his back against the couch.

"What are you doing?" Kaden yawned and climbed onto the couch. He sat cross-legged on the cushion behind Ryan. Gently, he wriggled his toe against the back of Ryan's head.

Ryan patted the box beside him and raised the tape gun. "Thought I'd lend a hand."

Kaden rubbed his eyes. "You don't have to."

Ryan reached behind him and squeezed Kaden's big toe. "I want to. I mean it's for me, right?"

Kaden chuckled. "Let's say it's for both of us and call it even."

"Deal." Ryan smoothed his hand over the tape, sealing the cardboard box. He then picked up a marker and wrote a brief note of what was inside along with *living room* in block capitals.

"I'm going to miss this place," Kaden said and stared out the window, his focus drawn to the section of river in the view.

"If you're having second thoughts—" He shut up

when Kaden nudged his shoulder. "I know. I know. I guess I need to pinch myself at times to make sure it's all real." He leaned back his head and met Kaden's eyes. "Strange to think about how things were back then, right?" He smiled when Kaden stroked his jaw.

Both he and Ryan had come so far in the last two years. Ryan had survived Paul and had come out stronger. The fallout had been manageable, and as much as Kaden hated Paul and everything he was, he couldn't help but be grateful for the sliver of decency that Paul had shown in the end. Advised by his lawyers to avoid the full-blown media circus of a trial, Paul had pleaded guilty, meaning everybody involved could start moving forward.

It wasn't only Ryan who pinched himself from time to time. Because of Ryan, Kaden had finally opened his heart again, had been able to trust someone, connect.

"I have no regrets," Kaden said. "Do you know how ridiculously happy I was when you asked me to move to LA with you?"

"You just liked the idea of being near the ocean."

Kaden grinned as he nodded. "True."

Ryan pouted, and Kaden pinched his cheek.

"Are you still okay with it all? Last chance to change your mind; no takebacks after today."

Ryan smiled, brushed the side of his head against the palm of Kaden's hand. "I'm not taking it back, and neither are you. We're stuck with each other from here on out."

"Sounds good to me." He bent down, tilted back Ryan's head, and stole a kiss. "You, me, and the ocean. Perfect."

Ryan reached up for another kiss. "Yes, it is."

---

Get the next book here - **Gideon**

### Gideon (Boyfriend for Hire 3)
#### Gideon

**A snowy cabin with one bed? That's only the first step toward Gideon falling in love.**

Gideon is too old to be fought over at Christmas by divorced parents who should know better. The prospect of a Christmas on his own is better than having to face either of them. When Rowan hires him for a wintery break in Maine, it seems like a safe choice until his PA's meddling family shows him something entirely new: Love.

Rowan hiring his boss for a trip back to his moms' place for Christmas sounded like a good idea at the time. Killing two birds with one stone, he can cheer up Gideon and possibly steal a kiss under the mistletoe. After all, he's been hiding his attraction to the man for years, and maybe with some Christmas magic, he can help Gideon see what is right under his nose.

## Sapphire Cay

### Sapphire Cay

1. Follow the Sun
2. Under the Sun
3. Chase The Sun
4. Christmas In The Sun
5. Capture The Sun
6. Forever In The Sun

## Also from RJ & Meredith

### Standalone Christmas

- <u>The Road to Frosty Hollow</u>

### Free Reads

- Stronger Together

## Meet RJ Scott

RJ discovered romance in books at a very young age and realized that if there wasn't romance on the page, she could create it in her head. With over one hundred and fifty books published, she is a full time author of gay romance.

She lives and works out of her home in the beautiful English countryside, spends her spare time reading, watching films, and enjoying time with her family.

The last time she had a week's break from writing she didn't like it one little bit and has yet to meet a box of chocolates she couldn't defeat.

www.rjscott.co.uk | rj@rjscott.co.uk

**NEWSLETTER - rjscott.co.uk/rjnews**

facebook.com/author.rjscott

instagram.com/rjscott_author

amazon.com/author/rj-scott

bookbub.com/authors/rj-scott

goodreads.com/rjscott

patreon.com/RJScott

## Meet Meredith Russell

Meredith Russell lives in the heart of England. An avid fan of many story genres, she enjoys nothing less than a happy ending. She believes in heroes and romance and strives to reflect this in her writing. Sharing her imagination and passion for stories and characters is a dream Meredith is excited to turn into reality.

www.meredithrussell.co.uk
meredithrussell666@gmail.com

 facebook.com/meredithrussellauthor

X x.com/MeredithRAuthor

 instagram.com/miss_meredith_r